THE HIDDEN TREASURE OF THE FORGOTTEN PHARAOH

Lee Ann Thomas

iUniverse, Inc.
New York Bloomington

The Hidden Treasure of the Forgotten Pharaoh

iUniverse books may be ordered through booksellers or by contacting:

iUniverse
1663 Liberty Drive
Bloomington, IN 47403
www.iuniverse.com
1-800-Authors (1-800-288-4677)

ISBN: 978-0-595-47552-0 (pbk)
ISBN: 978-0-595-71157-4 (cloth)
ISBN: 978-0-595-91820-1 (ebk)

Printed in the United States of America

iUniverse Rev. Date 11/12/08

To my wonderful family for all their
love and support.
To my students
Juan, Nikki, and Esmeralda,
who inspired the characters of this book.
But most of all to my loving sister, Cindy,
who gave me the faith, courage, and
ability to chase my dreams.

Author's Note

▼

Queen Hatshepsut, of the Eighteenth Dynasty, was an incredible woman. She was the oldest daughter of Pharaoh Tuthmosis I, and she married her half brother, Tuthmosis II. Upon the death of Tuthmosis II, the throne of Egypt passed out of Queen Hatshepsut's immediate possession and into the hands of the young male child of a secondary wife of Tuthmosis II. The queen, feeling that the male child, Tuthmosis III, was too young to reign as pharaoh over all of Egypt, decided to become the guardian of the young pharaoh and co-rule with him. Once in power, she declared herself to be pharaoh by the right of divine birth as the daughter of Tuthmosis I.

She defied tradition by establishing herself on the divine throne as a female pharaoh. She dressed in male clothing and even wore the pharaoh's traditional false beard. Her reign was one of peace, prosperity, monument building, and foreign exploration. The great Temple of Deir el-Bahri was in fact built by Senenmut as Queen Hatshepsut's mortuary temple and is located on the western side of the Nile River, situated magnificently at the foot of sheer cliffs that fringe the desert hills.

After Queen Hatshepsut's death, Tuthmosis III did in fact make a serious attempt to destroy her memory from the annals of Egyptian history. Her monuments were destroyed or defaced, her pictures were vandalized, and her name was chiseled off walls, temples, and obelisks. For more than two thousand years, her name truly was forgotten.

CHAPTER ONE

▼

Squinting his eyes against the glare of the sun, fifteen-year-old Nikki Weston watched as the sun bore down upon the sands of the desert around him. Turning, he saw in the distance some hills rising in the west. He pulled his cap lower. For a week, his parents had allowed him and his tutor to explore the ruins of ancient Egypt while they attended to their business in Luxor.

Every day, Nikki and his tutor spent their time wandering the ruins only to return each night to give an account to his parents of what Nikki had seen and learned. Nikki felt cramped by this constant questioning and longed to be free of his family's expectation that he would one day take over their antiquity business and huge family estate in Scotland.

Nikki wanted to be the discoverer of the ancient antiquities that his father bought from the local dealers. He wanted to be the one to find the priceless hidden relics, not like his father, who purchased them to sell to private collectors or museums. This was his greatest wish, and Egypt was a perfect place to explore this dream.

Most of his dream and his sense of adventure had come from his tutor. After having been kicked out of numerous private schools for pulling practical jokes, his family had resorted to hiring a series of private tutors. However, his lack of discipline and constant joking had caused all of his tutors to quit within the first few weeks. But finally his father had found the perfect one. It was considered odd, to say the least, in 1896, that a wealthy British young man would have a young adult woman tutor, but his father cared only about what worked, not about what others thought.

At first Nikki had been skeptical and had played numerous jokes on his new female tutor. However, her unfailing patience and warmhearted and open ways soon dissolved his selfish, undisciplined behavior, and they became fast friends rather than a tutor and a student.

Her name was Amanda Tilson, but Nikki affectionately called her Tiggy after his favorite stuffed childhood toy. She had been doing work in the Egyptian section of the British National Museum when her patron suddenly died, leaving her with no money to continue her research on some ancient Egyptian scrolls from the Eighteenth Dynasty. There were plenty of jobs available for a young, attractive twenty-five-year-old woman in London, England, but none that respectable, intelligent young women like Amanda would consider. Therefore, she jumped at the chance to become a private tutor to the child of a wealthy family.

It was from Tiggy that Nikki had heard fantastic stories of adventure. She had helped awaken the adventurous spirit in his blood. While they were exploring the chambers of the tomb of Ramses II's sons, Tiggy had spoken of a hidden treasure, murder, intrigue, and the rumored sacred stones of Queen Hatshepsut. His mind reeled with the possibilities. He was eager to leave the dark, dusty, and creepy tombs to begin searching for clues about the ancient story.

"Nikki! Nikki!" he suddenly heard Tiggy shouting as she ran down the long narrow corridor of the tomb.

Throwing down a handful of hot sand, he jumped to his feet and began running toward the sound of her excited voice.

"I'm coming, Tiggy! Hold on!"

Tiggy emerged from the low tomb opening with great excitement written clearly on her face.

"Nikki!" she shouted. "Come quickly! I can't believe it! Come on! Hurry!"

"What! What is it?" he exclaimed as she practically dragged him back into the tomb.

"Wait! Just wait. I have to show you," she declared in her excitement as they walked along a narrow corridor covered with the sand and dust of a time long ago. Lowering her voice, she then whispered, "I can't tell you aloud, because even the walls have ears here."

Minutes later, the torch flickered over a small, empty eight-foot-by-eight-foot room. The walls were covered with hieroglyphics from floor to ceiling. It was silent and dark except for the light coming from the flaming torch. The air was stale and hot, and the floor was covered with a thick dense layer of sand. The low ceiling allowed for the torchlight to illuminate the entire room with little effort.

Nikki could hear the sound of something scurrying across the sandy floor as Tiggy walked toward the far wall, but chose to ignore it.

Look!" Tiggy crowed with triumph as she waved the torch toward the highly decorated and faded painted wall filled with scenes of Egyptian life and hieroglyphic stories.

"Look at what?" Nikki asked flippantly. "It's just an old dusty wall."

"Old wall nothing!" she returned in disbelief while brushing a cobweb from out of her face. "It speaks of the hidden treasure of Queen, I mean *Pharaoh* Hatshepsut. Look way down here, buried in the sand. See, I dug this part of the floor out and found this inscription separate from the rest of the drawings."

Nikki bent down close to the sand while Tiggy held the torch low.

"Do you see?" she cried with excitement.

"No!" he returned with disappointment.

"Look here!" she said as she knelt down and pointed to the small hieroglyphic inscription that looked like drawings of birds, ropes, flowers, bugs, and other objects still partially buried in the sand.

"It talks here of the sacred stone. In all my research, the stone of auta is only mentioned in reference to Hatshepsut's wealth. Before she died, she had her trusted servant, Hapuseneb, hide her wealth from Tuthmosis III."

Nikki listened intently now, even though he had heard the story many times.

"It's written that she knew of her nephew's hatred and chose to take the wealth of Egypt with her into the afterlife," Tiggy continued. "Her servant was said to be very loyal to her as well as crafty. It's rumored that he decided to hide her wealth where only the bravest could find it. Many have tried, yet no one has ever found it. These small hieroglyphics says that the auta is one of the important clues to the map. I've read that there were clues, but there never seemed to be anything written about what they were. Hmm ..." Tiggy paused, deep in thought.

"Surely a piece of papyrus wouldn't have survived since 1458 BC," declared Nikki with evident disbelief.

"Maybe not, but remember, Nikki, this is ancient Egypt we are talking about. Not everything is what it appears to be. They thought very differently than we do today," she wisely declared. "Come—it's getting late. The shadows are beginning to fall, and it's not wise to be caught in the desert at night."

"Tiggy," began Nikki on their way out of the tomb led only by the light of the flickering torch, "let's come back tomorrow and look for more clues."

"There's no reason why we cannot, since your parents are eager for you to learn as much as possible about ancient artifacts," she began, when suddenly the torch was blown out by a strong, moaning, hot wind.

"What's that?" asked Nikki in fear.

"Stay against the wall," whispered Tiggy. "Now! Stay out of the wind! Something must be coming toward us!"

"What?" he questioned, now petrified.

"Don't ask what! Just do it!"

Quickly the wind washed over them again, and Nikki grabbed on to Tiggy's arm with evident fear.

They heard the moaning again, but this time it was louder and nearer.

"It sounds like a voice," he whispered in a scared and shaky voice.

"Shh. It is saying something to us. Listen!"

A faint, raspy voice could be heard: "Now it begins ... find the auta ... beware of many ... trust few."

The wind stopped blowing as quickly as it had started.

They stood flat against the tomb wall, their breath shallow and their hearts racing.

"Did you understand what it said?" Nikki said at last with a squeak in his voice.

Hesitantly, Tiggy began with a shaky voice too, "Yes, it said that we had to start with the auta. But where are we to begin? There must be hundreds of autas around Egypt."

"Well, come on then," he said as he grabbed her hand, wanting to get out of the tomb as quickly as possible. "Let's get out of here because this place is giving me the creeps now."

Slowly, through the dark narrow passageways, they made their way out by running their hands along the walls until finally they reached the small opening of the tomb. The sun rays grew longer on the horizon as they made their way back toward the camels, their mode of transportation for desert travel. At first, Nikki had refused to ride on the smelly beast, but Tiggy told him that even though they were stinky and spit on you, they were still the best way to travel across the hot sands.

While riding their camels during the hour-long journey back to Luxor, Nikki asked, "Tiggy, what exactly are we looking for? I mean, I think I know, but I'm not quite sure."

"Good question," she replied. "You probably know that *auta* is the ancient Egyptian name for a cobra in a striking position. It was used on the crowns of all pharaohs. I think tomorrow we need to search for more clues in the same room we were in today. I wonder ..." Tiggy paused in midthought.

"Do you mean," cried out Nikki, "that there might be clues about where to start looking hidden on the walls of that tomb?"

"Shh!" admonished Tiggy. "Not so loud." She nodded toward their guide. "We don't want any of the workers to know what we are trying to find."

"Yeah," he said quietly. "No one—especially not my parents, because I want to find this treasure on our own without my father hiring an archaeologist to do it for us," he declared, throwing a challenging look toward her.

Tiggy stared at him for several moments and finally said, "Well, for now, there's nothing to tell. We're just busy learning from the sights of the ancient ruins."

Nikki let out a sigh of relief. He was thankful that Tiggy was not going to tell his parents of their new discovery just yet. He knew instinctively that his father would take over immediately and his adventure would be over.

He could tell by the look on Tiggy's face that she was trying hard to recall all that she knew of the auta of Hatshepsut. She was so deep in thought that she was allowing the camel to wander crazily across the desert floor.

Finally, he went over and grabbed the camel's rope, saying over his shoulder, "You keep on thinking, and I'll drive this smelly beast."

Dinner was a rather quiet affair that night back at the hotel in Luxor, with just Nikki and Tiggy dining; Nikki's parents had decided to eat later in the evening with a business associate of his father's. Nikki watched as Tiggy pored silently over dusty volumes of ancient Egyptian folklore. Occasionally he would tell her to eat, for she was so absorbed in what she was reading that her dinner had grown cold.

Nikki was becoming bored with this unusual silence and begged her to put away her books.

"Tiggy, you have not touched a thing on your plate," said a voice from behind them.

With no apparent interest in the speaker's identity, she reached out and touched the food with her fingers, saying, "There ... I touched it."

Nikki started to laugh as he rose to his feet and reached out to shake hands with the tall, handsome newcomer.

"Ian!" Nikki said. "Good to see you! I didn't know that you were in Luxor."

Ian threw Tiggy a questioning sidelong glance while reaching out to shake Nikki's hand.

"What's this, Tiggy? No greeting from you?" Ian joked while pulling the book out of her hand.

"Huh?" she said. As she looked up, her face broke into a wide smile.

"Ian!" she said, setting aside her things to greet him. She gave him a hug while Nikki drew another chair up to their table. "I never thought that you would come to Luxor."

"Well, things got a little boring in Scotland after you left. I got in contact with your steward, and he gave me directions to your hotel in Cairo. When I couldn't find you there, I came to the hotel he told me about here in Luxor. So, here I am, like it or not."

"This is great! Just what we needed," said Nikki with evident delight.

Ian was a neighbor of Nikki's parents back in Scotland. He had a rather large estate that bordered Nikki's father's, and Ian had been a part of Nikki's life since Nikki was old enough to toddle behind him when Ian was a mere sixteen-year-old. Now he was thirty-two, and his family had begun to bother him about settling down and starting a family. For the first time since Tiggy's arrival at the Weston estate, he actually began to think that maybe they were right; maybe it was time.

It was well-known that Ian was extremely wealthy and could jaunt from place to place without worrying about the expense. Therefore, it was no real surprise to either of them that he had found his way to Egypt. The three of them shared a close friendship and a strong bond, and to Nikki it seemed that the trip was now complete with his arrival.

It was with great enthusiasm that Nikki told Ian of their plans for the following day.

"Sounds like it's a challenge that has been eluding people for centuries. How do you plan to go about finding it?" asked Ian when Nikki finally stopped talking long enough to breathe.

"We—" began Tiggy, but Nikki interrupted.

"Why, with Tiggy, of course," he said. "She knows practically everything about Egypt."

"Not quite," interposed Tiggy.

"Well, you definitely have enough books in which to search for clues." Ian waved toward the pile on the table. "What did you do? Check out the whole Egyptian section in the library?"

"No," she said with mock indignation.

"Oh, this is nothing," Nikki said with a laugh. "You should see our rooms."

"If it is all right with Tiggy," said Ian with a questioning look at her.

"Sure, but only if you help carry these books," she replied.

Ian let out a low whistle when they arrived at their suite of rooms on the highest floor of the hotel. The rooms were wide and tall with beautiful white walls that made one feel cool just looking at them. The huge glass windows were open to allow for the maximum amount of air to cool the room. The handles and mirrors were all made of gold, and the sofas and chairs featured silk cushions.

"Wow, look at this place!" Ian said. "It looks as if the pharaohs have returned."

"Nice, isn't it?" she said while setting her books on a low table next to a couch by the balcony doors. "We have half the floor, and Nikki's parents have the other half. It's much better than I expected."

"Where's your room?" asked Nikki as he opened the doors to the balcony to bring in more of the cool night air.

"Oh, it's way down on the second floor, and it's stifling hot in there, absolutely not a breath of air."

"Move up here," declared Nikki. "I've got two beds in my room."

Ian looked over to where Tiggy was standing out on the balcony.

Nikki, seeing his hesitation, said, "Don't worry about Tiggy. She won't mind."

"I don't know, Nikki. I mean, her room is across from yours, and I wouldn't want anyone to misunderstand my presence here. So, I think for now I'll just stay in my room downstairs—at least until it gets too hot."

Yawning, Tiggy came in from the balcony. "I'm beat, so I'm going to bed."

She hugged Nikki good-night and admonished him not to stay up too late talking, because they needed to get an early start in the morning. Turning to Ian, she said, "I'm so glad you came. See you at breakfast?"

"Try to keep me away," he said as he waved good-bye.

CHAPTER TWO

───────────── ▼ ─────────────

"Nikki," called Ian from the inside of the dark, sandy passageway, "did you bring the oil for the lantern in with you?"

"No, I'll go get it, though. Where is Tiggy?"

"She left about twenty minutes ago mumbling something."

"Well, it's not like her to be gone so long," said Nikki with a worried voice.

"She'll be okay, Nikki. She is not afraid of much of anything."

"Except snakes," grinned Nikki wickedly as he remembered how he had put one of his favorite snakes in Tiggy's bed when he first met her. "Blast it, I still miss that snake," he whispered as he thought of how she had beaten it to a pulp and left it in his room.

Soon Nikki came back with the lantern filled with oil. For some time, he and Ian took rubbings of the tomb walls. First Nikki wiped the dust and crawling bugs from the wall. Then Ian came up with a piece of thin paper about six inches square and placed it over the hieroglyphics on the wall. Using a dark piece of chalk, Ian rubbed firmly over the drawings, making an impression on the paper.

"You never know when we may need these," said Ian as he stood up to stretch.

"I wish I could have seen how these looked when they were actually carved in the stone and then painted," Nikki said as he put away his supplies. "They must have been incredible."

"Yes, they must have been awe-inspiring," agreed Ian, bending down to pick up the lantern.

"I'm hungry," complained Nikki. "When can we eat?"

"Gosh! Is it lunchtime already?" questioned Ian as he looked at his watch. "Yep, one o'clock, to be exact."

"What? It's that late?" Nikki threw down his supplies and began rushing down the narrow corridor, lantern in hand, before Ian had a chance to blink.

"What's wrong?" Ian called as he began running after Nikki.

"Tiggy!" he yelled over his shoulder. "She's been gone for over three hours. Something must have happened."

Ian, catching up to him, said, "Hold on. She probably got busy doing something and lost track of the time, just like we did."

"No, if she found something interesting, she would've come and gotten me."

Running from corridor to corridor, they searched—first the corridor on the right and then down to the left—but did not find Tiggy. Turning back around, they ran down the opposite corridor, to the left, and then down a slope to another corridor, but still there was no sign of Tiggy. Several minutes and five corridors later, they finally found her. She was deathly pale and lying unconscious in the sand.

"Oh my God!" they exclaimed simultaneously.

Bending down, Ian grabbed Tiggy's wrist and felt for a pulse. Ian, upon finding one, let out the breath that he had been holding.

"Thank God she's alive," sighed Nikki after Ian announced that he had found a steady beat beneath his fingers.

Ian took out his water and poured some onto his handkerchief. Kneeling, he put his arm underneath her shoulders and dabbed her face with the cool cloth.

She began to stir. Soon her eyelids fluttered open wide with fear, and she put her hand up to her forehead.

"Ouch! My head hurts," she exclaimed as she sat up.

Kneeling, Nikki held the lantern near her face. "You're bleeding," he said as he pointed to her forehead.

Reaching up, she touched the spot and said, "I'll be fine in just a minute."

"Can you tell us what happened?" asked Ian.

She hesitated and then said, "Yes, I think so." She thought hard for a moment and then began, "I thought I heard someone talking in the next corridor, so I went over to look. When I didn't see anyone, I just followed the sounds."

"Are you crazy?" exclaimed Ian. "What if there were bandits or robbers? You could've been killed."

"Well, I thought of that at first, but then I realized that I was following a sound, not a light. There's no way you can find your way through this maze of corridors without some kind of light."

Nikki grunted, "You should've come back and gotten me. Then I could have defended you before they had a chance to bust you in the head like they did."

"That's just it, Nikki. There was no one!"

Ian looked at Nikki and said, "I think she hit her head a little harder than we thought."

"Will you just wait and listen before declaring me crazy?" she said while rising to her feet.

Picking up one of the lanterns, she walked to the far wall of the corridor. Setting down the lantern, she pointed to a colorful painting on the wall of Egyptian soldiers carrying back their spoils from a war.

"I followed the voice to here, and then I heard what seemed to be talking coming from the wall. I tried to find an opening, but no luck. However, I did find what I think is a significant clue."

Tiggy paused long enough to look at her listeners' faces to see if they were interested enough for her to continue.

"Clue? What clue?" said Nikki with excitement.

"I decided to retrace my steps and come get you two when the voice grew louder, almost angry with my departure. Then that strong wind came rushing by, except this time I couldn't get out of the way. Then it felt like someone pushed me. I had dropped my lantern, and I didn't see the wall until I hit it. I don't remember anything else till I saw you."

"Who pushed you? Surely not the wind?" said Ian with evident disbelief.

Angry that he did not believe her, she said, "Fine! Don't believe me, but I know what happened. Besides, I dare you to prove I am wrong! Go look for footprints since you think I'm wrong."

Ian looked sheepishly at her and said, "No need to get mad. You've got to admit the story sounds unbelievable."

Immediately her anger vanished.

This is creepy, Tiggy," declared Ian. "I really don't think we need to be in here."

"You think there're robbers here?" said Nikki in a scared voice.

"Nonsense," retorted Tiggy.

"Are you sure about staying, Tiggy?" asked Ian.

"Certainly. Now let me tell you what I found."

"Yes," said Nikki, reassured with her confidence, "tell us what you found."

Pointing back to the relief on the wall, she said, "Look at this scene where they're carrying in all the wealth that they have captured from what appears to be the Nubians. If you follow the scene, you can see that the hieroglyphics are a little misshapen. If you stand further back"—she motioned them to follow her—"you can see that the irregular-shaped parts now become a new hieroglyphic. I was able to discern *Deir-el*, which I concluded stands for Deir-el-Bahari, which is the funeral temple for Queen Hatshepsut."

"Excellent!" shouted Nikki. "Now we know exactly where to begin."

"Not exactly," replied Ian, "because Deir-el-Bahari is a rather large temple. We could search for years and never find anything."

Tiggy continued to stare at the relief on the wall as Nikki and Ian argued about who would be the first to find the hidden auta.

"We'll see … we will just see," finished Nikki as he went to stand by Tiggy. "See something else?"

"Ooh, my head hurts, and these things are getting blurry."

"Let me try. Maybe I'll see something you missed," he said.

Ian joined them, and soon all three were concentrating on the ancient wall relief.

"Tiggy, look!" cried Nikki, running over to the relief and placing his hand on several different pictures. "Do you see what I see? It's the crook of the pharaoh!"

Ian and Tiggy quickly moved behind Nikki.

"You're right! It's another clue," stated Ian.

"Yes, it is," said Tiggy with enthusiasm. "See, Nikki, I told you that you could find clues too."

Happy to have found a clue, they began to look earnestly for more.

"Look, a lotus flower!" shouted Ian. "But the wall relief ends; the corridor turns, and there's nothing else."

"I wonder," began Tiggy, "if these clues are the only ones we are going to find. I would think that the high priest Hapuseneb, being so crafty, would've scattered the clues about more."

"Look at the top of the picture," Ian said. "It has eroded off."

"Or has been chipped off," added Nikki.

"You can see that it was the beginning of a cartouche, the royal seal that holds the name of the pharaoh," began Ian as a wind began to blow.

"The wind!" both Tiggy and Nikki cried out as they flattened themselves against the nearest wall.

"Against the wall, Ian!" yelled Nikki as the wind intensified.

"Where did the wind come from?" questioned Ian.

"Move!" Nikki commanded, but he was too late.

To their horror and awe, Nikki and Tiggy watched as Ian was lifted into the air as if by a person. They watched, frozen in fear, as Ian flipped and flopped in midair, screaming as the wind did with him what it wanted. His arms were flailing, and his legs were kicking. Finally the wind, as if tired of dealing with him, threw him down into the sand several feet away. The eerie sound of a voice was heard: "Believe!"

11

The wind left Ian and swirled around Nikki and Tiggy, saying, "Seek Deir-el-Bahari."

The wind ceased suddenly.

Nikki and Tiggy ran quickly over to where Ian was sprawled out facedown in the sand.

"Are you okay?" they questioned with voices full of panic as Ian rolled over and stared at them with wide eyes.

Slowly he nodded his head and whispered, "I didn't believe, but I do now."

Seeing that he was all right, Nikki now began laughing and mimicking Ian, for, having experienced the swirling wind before, he now found the strange phenomenon somewhat humorous, and it also helped him release the sense of fear that had been welling up within him.

"You should have seen yourself," he began as tears of laughter began to stream down his cheeks. "Your arms were flapping like chicken wings," he said as he lay down in the sand, laughing.

"Yes," joined in Tiggy. "You were flopping around like a fish out of water." Like Nikki, she was having a hard time controlling her mirth.

Sitting on the sand, they both kept laughing and imitating the way that Ian had been moving around in the air.

"Ha-ha," continued Nikki while flapping his arms. "It was the funniest damn thing I've seen in a while."

"All right," said Ian, now rising to his feet to brush off the sand. "It couldn't have been that funny."

"Oh, yes it was!" said Nikki, still laughing, as he lay back and began flapping his arms and kicking his feet while making chicken noises.

"Tiggy, make him stop!" complained Ian. "You're supposed to make him listen, not encourage him in this."

Unable to control her laughter, she just waved Ian away while wiping the tears from her eyes.

Finally, she realized that Ian was getting upset and made Nikki stop.

"Well," she said while rising from the ground and wiping the sand away, "at least we know where to start looking."

"How do you know that?" said Ian while picking up the tools.

"The wind," said Nikki.

"The wind?" questioned Ian.

"Yeah, but you were too busy to hear it," blurted out Nikki with renewed laughter.

Tiggy, breaking in, said, "All right, you two. We have more important things to do now than make fun of each other. So let's get busy collecting our tools and lanterns and get out of here."

Some fifteen minutes later, they exited the passageway and lifted their satchels containing their tools and water onto the backs of their waiting camels.

"Where are we headed?" Nikki asked Tiggy.

"That's what I was just wondering," she replied. "We could start now, even though it's already afternoon, or we could get a fresh start in the morning. What do you think?" she asked while looking at Nikki and Ian.

"I'm for starting now," answered Nikki.

"It really does not matter to me," said Ian. "Whatever you think is best."

"Well, I am for starting in the morning, because we need to get more food and water, number one, and number two, my head is killing me," she stated.

Turning toward her, Ian said, "Yeah, I can see why it would be. You have a gash on your head and a pretty large bruise. Why didn't you say something earlier?"

Shrugging, she replied, "I guess I was too caught up in the excitement of finding more clues to worry about the pain."

Looking at Tiggy, Nikki felt guilty for not considering her feelings. He decided not to insist that they go immediately to Deir-el-Bahari. Instead, he said, "You're right. We should get a good night's sleep and start fresh in the morning. Maybe you'll be feeling better by then."

Tiggy smiled gratefully at him. Just a few short months ago, he would have never thought of anyone's feelings but his own. She knew in her heart that he desperately wanted to begin that very day but was suppressing his wish because he had finally learned from her how to be unselfish.

Chapter Three

──────────── ▼ ────────────

The stars had not quite gone to sleep when the caravan left Luxor and headed toward the desert. Deir-el-Bahari, on the western shore of the river Nile opposite the ancient city of Thebes, was the destination, and Nikki, Tiggy, and Ian were eager to be off.

Nikki was, as usual, filled with anticipation of what he hoped to find and was talking excitedly to Ian. He was stunned that his parents had allowed him to embark on this journey, for he knew it would take them almost a day, by camel, to reach Deir-el-Bahari. He also knew that it was Tiggy's insistence that had convinced his parents, and it was she who had calmed their fears. He glanced at her and smiled.

Tiggy was quietly reading as her camel swayed beneath her. She was intently reading about the reign of Tuthmosis III, hoping to uncover information that they might find useful. Nikki knew, as did Tiggy, that she was still missing valuable pieces of information. But she had given up on encouraging him to read anything while he was talking with Ian.

By nightfall, the small caravan reached Deir-el-Bahari. It had been a hot but thankfully uneventful journey.

Ian told one of the workers to set up the tents for the night, while Tiggy instructed two of the others to begin cooking their supper. Nikki quickly placed rocks around the perimeter of a shallow pit he had dug in the sand. Taking wood from a pack on a camel's back, he soon had a large fire burning from the phosphorus-laden matches that Tiggy had made him carry in his satchel.

"We'll eat in about five minutes," announced Tiggy some thirty minutes later. "Nikki, come fix your bed and put your supplies in your tent for tonight."

Reluctantly, Nikki threw down the huge beetle he had been annoying and did as he was told.

After eating their small supper, which consisted mainly of fruits and a young goat, Ian decided to prepare his pistol and clean it, just in case.

Nikki threw a questioning look at Tiggy. "What's with the gun, or should I say *guns*?" he corrected as he saw Ian pull out another pistol. "Are we going into battle? Are we going to be shooting people?" he continued as he watched Ian unload a duffel bag full of weapons.

"No, we are not looking for a fight or going to be involved in one. We are just being prepared."

"Prepared for what?"

"Anytime you sleep in the desert at night, you must be prepared to repel bandits, if they attack," Tiggy replied. "Hence the reason I asked you to take your supplies into your tent. Some bandits steal only the camels, and some steal everything, but you never know. Don't you remember that your father told you that this could turn out to be more of an adventure than you might realize? That's one of the reasons why we have a few extra workers in the caravan. Your father wanted to protect us in the event that some bandits may try to approach our camp. "

"Oh," replied Nikki with surprise. "I never thought that there was a chance that we would be in a gunfight! This is great! A real live battle right here!"

"Not something that you want to be in the middle of," replied Ian, who had been silent up to this point.

"Why not? I'm not afraid to die," he remarked bravely.

"That's good, but what if I was killed, or even worse, what if Tiggy was? Then what?" posed Ian.

Nikki was silent for a moment as he pondered this hypothetical. Slowly he nodded his head. "I see what you mean. Do I get to use a gun too?" he questioned as he watched Ian hand Tiggy a pistol and a rifle.

"Yes, you do," was the reply. "You know how to shoot, so you need to protect yourself."

Tiggy stood and said, "I'm off to bed. Wake me up around 2 AM, when it's my turn."

"Turn for what?" questioned Nikki.

"My turn to watch for bandits," she replied as she walked toward her tent.

Dawn subtly caressed the sands of Egypt as it had for thousands of years, as Tiggy stood with her face to the rising warmth. In some ways, the land here still looked untouched by man, she thought as she gazed out across the sand-covered landscape toward the rising sun. The gentle breeze blew her hair across her shoulders and then became harsher while her thoughts took her back across the centuries. *Did someone long ago stand on this very spot and watch the same sunrise?* she wondered.

Suddenly her head pounded, and she felt dizzy. Closing her eyes to regain her balance and deal with the sharp pain in her forehead, she stood still for several minutes, allowing the breeze to rush over her. Upon opening her eyes, everything appeared rather blurry. She blinked in surprise when she saw that all around her the area was full of life and sounds. Confused, she looked around and noticed that everything appeared relatively new and that people were dressed in the costumes of the ancients. Bewildered, she could do nothing but stare at what was going on around her.

She saw women draped in common linen with kohl-darkened eyes, old and young men carrying heavy burdens to what appeared to be a marketplace, and a young boy carrying a basket much too large for his size, laden with dates; she heard the bleat of a goat and a laugh from a nearby woman.

A loud commotion suddenly drew her attention eastward. Spying a cloud of dust, she narrowed her eyes, only to behold what appeared to be a royal entourage coming closer.

Still numb with disbelief, she could only stand and stare. Seconds later, the entourage passed with what appeared to be a pharaoh and his royal subjects. Looking up, Tiggy gazed into the eyes of a beautiful young woman who had long black silky hair, skin the color of almonds, and high graceful cheekbones. She gave Tiggy a look of acknowledgment and mouthed, "I will help you. Come."

In disbelief, Tiggy looked over her shoulder, thinking that the young woman was mistaken. *Surely the woman is not talking to me. She clearly is confused,* mused Tiggy as she watched them pass. The young woman continued to stare at Tiggy, mouthing, "Come!" as the entire scene vanished beneath the sands of the desert.

Tiggy shook her head, closing her eyes as the pain returned and the breeze rushed over her once again.

Opening her eyes, she turned and saw the camp behind her, as she knew it should be. She could hear the workers making breakfast and getting ready for the day. The scene that had just been before her had disappeared as quickly as it had come. Her mind reeled with the possibility that she had received a vision from the past, a beckoning to come back through the centuries. Tiggy felt that for some reason the woman had recognized her; she knew that it was impossible, yet the feeling had definitely been there.

She was torn about whether to share what had occurred with the others. She was still standing in the same location when Nikki came to call her for breakfast several minutes later.

"Breakfast is ready."

Noticing her strange stare, Nikki quickly asked, "Are you okay? What's wrong?"

She gave a weak semblance of a smile. "Nothing, Nikki. Nothing at all."

He was sure she had not told him the truth, but he wisely let her have her own secrets.

At breakfast, Tiggy listened as Nikki and Ian planned the day.

"I think we should investigate the Shrine of Anubis on the right side of the corridor," said Nikki.

"I say we explore the Shrine of Hathor," disagreed Ian.

The two went back and forth, each arguing why his strategy for finding clues was better than the other's. Tired of their arguing, Tiggy gathered up her dishes and went to get her supplies for the day.

Coming back minutes later with her knapsack and canteen full of water, Ian and Nikki were still disagreeing with each other.

Stopping momentarily to look at them, she shook her head, turned, and began walking toward the massive stone temple that was carved magnificently into the hillside, with its large upward-sloping ramps and colossal stone columns. Both looked at her in surprise, asking, "Where are you going?"

She said over her shoulder, "I'm going to look for clues. You two can sit and argue all you want to, but I've got a treasure to find!"

Both scrambled to their feet and raced to get their knapsacks that held their tools, torches, oil, food, and a canteen of water. Tiggy continued toward the temple, not knowing exactly where to start. She sensed that she would know once she stepped into the temple.

"What's with leaving us?" asked Nikki flippantly.

Raising her eyebrows at his tone, she paused and then replied, "If you want to waste time arguing, that is your prerogative, but I don't want to be included in such childish behavior that will succeed in getting us nowhere. I'm sick of you two arguing. Have either one of you read books about this temple or its history?"

Nikki shook his head.

"So how do you both think you know where to begin?" she asked. "Well, I have read and have done the research, so stop arguing and let's go."

Ian had the sense to be embarrassed for arguing like a child, but Nikki remained petulant that Tiggy had left without him.

Clearing his throat, Ian said, "So what do we look for first?"

"I say we look for all the clues," ventured Nikki.

"You're exactly right," said Tiggy with a smile. "We have no idea where to find what; therefore we have to have the presence of mind to be constantly looking for all of the symbols."

"The pharaoh's crook, the lotus flower, and the auta itself," Ian said.

"What do you think the auta will be?" asked Nikki.

"Maybe on a relief?" questioned Ian.

"I don't think so," began Tiggy. "What I have read, in various texts, leads me to believe that it'll be something else. What else, I have no idea, for the descriptions were rather vague."

As the trio walked up the first of the three main corridors, each was awestruck at the sheer size of the temple. It towered stories above them like the hillside it was built into; the width of the columns exceeded the length of their fully extended arms, from fingertip to fingertip. Despite the ravages of time, the temple still revealed the magnificence of ancient Egypt.

Finally, Nikki seemed to find his breath. "This place must have been incredible during its time!" Running up the rest of the ramp, he burst into the first main hallway. "Wow! This is beautiful!" he said, unable to contain his excitement.

Tiggy and Ian watched as Nikki ran from wall to wall, exclaiming over every carving on every column and every painting that he saw and what remained of the ancient tiles on the floor. Tiggy smiled to herself as she watched his mounting enthusiasm with each new item that he beheld.

Suddenly, he stopped. Standing against the far wall, he gazed upon a large carving in the stone, depicting what he imagined was an important story from Egyptian history, to the right of the main corridor. "Hey, you two … hurry up and look at this."

Tiggy and Ian hastened their steps to catch up with him.

Ian let out a low whistle, and Tiggy exclaimed softly, "It's a beautiful wall relief. Look at how the detail of the carving has lasted all these thousands of years. It's a shame that the paint has not lasted through the centuries."

"Can you read what it says?" asked Ian.

"Yes, hmm, let me see," she said as she ran her hand gently over the carved hieroglyphics at the bottom of the scene on the wall. She stood quietly for several minutes before she began to speak.

"These are telling a story about the painting, about how the pharaoh—Hatshepsut, I believe, because the cartouche is chiseled off—sent explorers to the mysterious land of Punt. The journey was thousands of miles long. It says here that the queen of Punt returned to Egypt with gold, cinnamon, clove, and exotic trees. Hmm …" She paused as she ran her fingers along the wall, trying to discern the carved shape on the hieroglyphic.

With no warning, a pain shot through her head, causing her to cry out. She staggered and fell away from the wall relief.

"What is it?" cried Ian and Nikki with alarm.

But she did not respond. She just held her hands to her head. Not getting a response, they each grabbed an arm and shook her.

With great strength, she pulled away from them and stepped back against the far wall. All Ian and Nikki could do was watch and wait.

The pain subsided, and Tiggy could see that the wall relief in front of her had changed to brilliant colors. Glancing to the left and right, she noticed that the corridor had changed in appearance too. It was no longer dusty and filled with crumbling rock but was composed of marble floors and gilded walls beautifully decorated with various scenes.

"You came," said a voice behind her, causing Tiggy to start and turn abruptly around.

She saw the beautiful young woman with the beautiful black hair and the almond-colored skin from her earlier vision. Hesitantly, she asked, "You know me?"

"Yes, I have been waiting."

"You have?" questioned Tiggy with disbelief.

"Listen … there is not much time. You must find the stone and come to me in person."

"You know where the stone is?"

"I know where the clues are to lead you to the stone."

"Why do you want me to come to you?"

"Because you're my only hope."

"Hope of what?"

"I have not the time to explain," exclaimed the woman with impatience. "Quickly, you must go to the garden and find the lotus at the base of the statue of Tuthmosis I. When you find it, you alone must touch the flower and pull it free from the stone. Next, go to the Temple of Hatshepsut through the upper colonnade. Upon entering, turn to the right. The third column will have a hieroglyphic of the lotus; place the piece you find there. The lotus will lead you to the crook." Pausing, she looked at Tiggy. "You must hurry! I will be waiting."

"How do you know all of this? Why do you need me to come quickly?"

"No questions. There is not the time. Just come!" she said as she faded into the wall.

"No, wait!" Tiggy called out as she reached to grasp the young woman. The pain shot through her head, and she reeled back against the wall. Opening her eyes, Tiggy knew that she had returned. Exhausted from the ordeal, she sank down upon the sand.

Looking up, she saw the shocked faces of Nikki and Ian. Ian bent down, softly asking, "Are you all right?"

"What was that all about?" blurted out Nikki.

Looking at their concerned faces, she decided to tell them what she had experienced.

"What did you see and hear?" she asked gingerly.

"After you screamed, we tried to get you to say something, but you just pulled away. I must say, I never realized how strong you were," said Ian with amazement.

"Then, we just had to watch you as you began saying really strange things," added Nikki.

"How strange?" she asked.

"Well, you didn't seem to be making any sense, but Ian finally determined that you were speaking some form of ancient Egyptian."

"Tiggy, you must tell us what is going on," pleaded Ian.

"I am seeing things, visions I guess," she replied while anxiously watching their faces.

"Visions?" both Nikki and Ian repeated.

"I don't know what else to call them. I have no warning before they come, just a severe pain, where I injured my head, and then everything is transformed back to its original form." "Are you serious?" asked Nikki.

"How many of these have you had?" questioned Ian.

"This was the second. I had one right before breakfast while I was standing, looking out over the desert."

"So that's why you looked so weird when I came to tell you that breakfast was ready," Nikki said.

"Yes. I had just come out of it and was still somewhat confused."

"What did you see in these visions?" inquired Ian.

She recapped what she had seen and what she had been told in both visions.

"This is fantastic!" cried Nikki. "It means that now we have a place to start looking."

"You don't actually think that there is anything to these, do you?" said Ian in disbelief.

Tiggy began to pace the corridor and finally stopped, saying, "I have to, Ian. It was so real. The woman told me exactly where to find the first clue and where to place it to find the second."

"You are sure?"

"Yes, absolutely! She was very specific, and she also told me that I needed to hurry and come to her." Tiggy paused, thinking. "What she meant by that I have no idea, but we'll deal with that later."

Nikki broke in, saying, "Well, I'm for going to find the first clue."

"You're serious, aren't you?" said Ian.

"Well, there's only one way to find out if she is right and if what is happening is real. Let's go find the statue of Tuthmosis I out in what used to be the royal garden," said Tiggy with a hint of excitement.

CHAPTER FOUR

───────── ▼ ─────────

"Hello, Tuthmosis, you old man," cried Nikki as he spotted the large stone statue of the once-great pharaoh lying partially broken on the ground. Looking at the statue, Ian said, "I don't see how this is going to do us any good. It's broken in half, and one of its arms is missing. And you can't even read all of the hieroglyphics on the base."

Tiggy was not really paying attention to Ian; she was too busy looking at the gardens, which were in ruins. In the center, she saw what appeared to be the remains of a bathing pool. Broken pieces of small columns and stone tiles were flung across the sand, which at one time must have been a covered patio of sorts.

"Tiggy, the statue?" reminded Nikki.

"Oh, yes. Well, it doesn't matter that it's broken," stated Tiggy as she pushed in between the two of them. "The woman told me that the lotus was on the base of the statue," she said while lying down and looking underneath the statue, "that all I needed to do was to pull it free."

"Pull it out?" asked a confused Nikki. "How are you going to pull it out of stone?"

"Here ... turn him over," said Tiggy as she wiped the sand off her face as she sat back on her heels. "I saw the lotus symbol on the side facing the ground."

With great effort, the three of them pushed and pulled and pushed some more until finally the statue rolled onto its opposite side.

"See, there it is, plain as day," said Tiggy proudly. Kneeling down, she placed her hands upon the lotus, unsure of what to expect. Ian and Nikki

21

eagerly gathered around to watch and see if what she had described would come to pass.

Tiggy felt the lotus flower grow warm beneath her touch, and it began to glow. Not moving her hands, she looked up and smiled at Ian, saying, "We did it! The vision was true."

She smiled as she felt the piece come loose in her hands. She gently pulled the piece free, amazed at its beauty and detail. It was no larger than four inches in length, about one-fourth inch thick, and three inches in width, and it was made of pure gold. Each petal of the flower was adorned with precious stones, which appeared to be diamonds. The green leaves and stem were also decorated in the same way, except with emeralds. The piece was rectangular in shape but had a curious rounded piece jutting out of the right side.

It was an incredible artifact, truly a sight to behold. A master craftsman did the workmanship—that much was obvious. Amazingly, it had survived through the centuries with nary a scratch.

Standing with a look of triumph, she held it out to Nikki and Ian. Each in turn held the lotus, marveling at its beauty. Ian noticed that when he handed the piece back to Tiggy, the gold seemed to glow under her touch.

Bending down, she brushed the sand off her trousers, saying, "Let's go find the second clue."

"How about lunch first?" asked Ian as they trekked back across the ancient garden. Nikki seconded Ian's suggestion.

"If that is what you two wish, yes. I did not eat half my breakfast with all the arguing that was going on around me," she said with a smile.

Turning toward base camp, Nikki asked, "What did the temple look like when you saw it in your vision?"

"It was like nothing I have ever seen, so beautiful. It was incredible. It was so grand, just like how an artist would depict it in a book. At first, I was speechless when I saw the woman."

"I wish I could have seen it," said Nikki morosely.

"So do I, but without the pain that took me there."

Lunch was quiet, none wanting to discuss the finding in front of the workers for fear they might try to steal what the trio had found, as there was such a large market for Egyptian antiquities. They talked of commonplace things, the weather, traveling, food, and the like, nothing that would be of any interest to anyone who might be eavesdropping on their conversation.

After lunch, Nikki went to refill their canteens from the large water bags tied to one of the camels while Tiggy and Ian added a few additional supplies to their knapsacks. Finally they were ready to embark on their second journey into the great stone temple.

Excitement was running high as they journeyed up the ramp toward the Temple of Hatshepsut. Nikki and Tiggy were eager to learn if what the woman in the vision had said was true, while Ian remained hesitant.

"Just think—in a matter of minutes, we might have the next clue," crowed Nikki with evident delight.

"Yes, exciting, isn't it?" replied Tiggy, her eyes shining.

"Wonderful," mumbled Ian.

Both stopped and looked at Ian in surprise.

"What's wrong?" asked Nikki. "Why don't you want to look for the next clue?"

"Maybe I'm scared."

Tiggy and Nikki stopped walking and stood completely still. Shock and confusion registered on their faces. Tiggy walked to stand beside Ian and placed her hand on his arm; looking up, she asked, "Why are you afraid?"

"I am afraid for you, not for me."

"Me?" exclaimed Tiggy with surprise. "Whatever for?"

Looking down into her face, he simply stated, "I don't like the fact that you have these painful visions. It's not worth it for some ancient treasure that might never be found."

"Ian, I can't control them. They'll come whether I want them to or not."

"I know. That's what's bothering me. You can't control what's happening."

"But can any of us truly control a situation?" came her gentle reply.

"Yes, we can control some things to a certain degree."

"That's true, and that's exactly what I thought we were trying to do. We're going to find these pieces and soothe the troubled spirit of this young woman who keeps appearing. You'll see, Ian; things have a way of working themselves out."

Ian looked down at her, amazed at her determination and calm despite all the things that had happened to her lately. After taking a deep breath, he agreed that he would support the continuation of the adventure.

"Come on, Ian," complained Nikki. "Nothing is going to happen to Tiggy. Besides, we're closer than ever to finding the second clue."

"This is true," said Tiggy with a smile. "In fact, it's just up ahead. The young woman said to find the upper colonnade and the third column on the right. Don't worry, Ian. You'll see. We'll be all right."

Tiggy gave him an encouraging smile and walked on ahead.

Ian followed her and Nikki with his eyes. With a shrug of his shoulders, he followed them.

"Now what?" shouted Nikki in dismay. "There's no lotus flower on this column."

"I don't know," responded Tiggy, somewhat confused. "I remember her saying the third column on the right. I don't understand."

"Do you think that they could have moved one of these columns over the centuries?" asked Nikki.

"Not likely," chimed in Ian. "These look to hold a large section of this part of the roof. I wouldn't imagine that they would move the whole thing without the roof tumbling down."

"Well, let's just look at all the columns in this corridor," said Tiggy with a sigh. "Maybe one of them will have the carving of the lotus flower."

"Stupid!" exclaimed Nikki while slapping his forehead. "Stupid! How could we be so stupid?"

"What?" they chorused.

"Ancient hieroglyphics are read top to bottom and left to right. So maybe the woman gave us the directions according to how she read."

"Excellent!" declared Tiggy. "Let's try the third column up, not to the right!"

But Nikki was already there as the words left her mouth.

"Yes! It's here, near the bottom of the column."

The closer Tiggy came to the column, the warmer the lotus flower became. She had taken it out of her shirt and now held it in her hand. It glowed as she drew nearer and nearer. She marveled at its brilliance and cautiously bent down to place it on the hieroglyphic on the stone column.

Immediately the golden flower seemed to take on a life of its own, pulling itself toward the carved stone as a light poured forth. Tiggy could feel the energy pulsating up her arm as she at last held the lotus piece against the column. The feelings intensified as she continued to hold it, not knowing what to do next.

"What now?" asked Ian.

"I don't know. The woman just said it would show me the way."

"And show us it did! Look!" cried Nikki. "Look at that far column! It is beginning to open."

Everyone looked up, their eyes wide with astonishment.

"Incredible!" whispered Ian.

"Come on! Let's go before it closes! It has to lead to the other clues," said Nikki, already halfway there.

Ian bent down and picked up the rest of the gear while Tiggy continued to hold the flower in place.

"Hurry, Tiggy! This thing might close on us," yelled Nikki.

"I can't break free! The flower is holding me here. My hand can't break loose. Go ... just go! I must be needed to hold the column open."

Ian gave one last look over his shoulder before entering the secret passageway with Nikki.

"Wait, Nikki. We need to light the way! We've no idea what we're getting into. Let's at least see our way through this."

"What about Tiggy? We can't just leave her."

"She has to stay behind to keep the door open, Nikki. I don't like it either, but what choice do we have?"

Nikki hesitated and then finally turned away from the opening to glance around the inside of a narrow passageway. Before them, a winding staircase spiraled downward; there was nothing else inside the small space. Having no other alternative, they began to walk down the stairs with lanterns held high.

They were halfway down when they heard Tiggy's piercing scream and the rumble of the door as it began to close behind them.

"No!" they shouted in unison while running back up the stairs.

"Tiggy! Tiggy!" yelled Ian as he pounded on the stone door. "Tiggy, can you hear me? Answer me!"

Their pounding was met with silence as each looked at the other with dismay.

"Now what?" demanded Nikki.

"I don't know. Just let me think."

Nikki put his ear against the stone and listened. He heard another faint scream. "Ian, we've got to get out of here. Something is happening to Tiggy!"

"I know!" he shouted while pushing against the heavy stone door. "There's no way to move this thing."

Nikki stood with his ear to the door, listening intently. He could hear nothing but the pounding of his own heart. "Come on, Ian. Do something! You're supposed to know what to do."

"I could use some help here, if you don't mind, not criticism!"

The door began to groan and opened slowly. As soon as it opened a crack, Nikki slid through and went to find Tiggy.

"What was all that screaming about?" he demanded when he saw her holding the flower in place on the column.

"You don't want to know!" she replied weakly. "It was terrible, the worst thing that I have ever seen, and I hope to never have such a vision again."

"You certainly scared us half to death," stated Ian as he ran up behind her.

"I'm really sorry. It's not like I knew that you could even hear me."

"What happened?" said Ian anxiously.

"I was just sitting there holding the lotus in place when the pain came, only this time the pain was excruciating and the vision was terrifying." She

25

trembled at the remembrance of what she had seen. "I really don't want to talk about it. Please, just continue searching, and I'll hold the door open as long as I can."

"Why don't you just rest," suggested Ian.

She shook her head. "No, I am fine. I can do this."

"Something is obviously trying to scare us off," Ian said. "Therefore, we'll go in, and you close the door behind us. Every fifteen minutes or so, you open the passageway and see if we have returned. If not, just close it up again for another fifteen minutes."

After contemplating what he had said, she finally agreed.

Ian reached over and touched her on the shoulder. "It's okay. Don't worry about scaring us. I mean, I needed a couple of gray hairs to look a little bit older than thirty-two anyway."

Looking up, she smiled as she watched them disappear through the door into the hidden passageway.

CHAPTER FIVE

—————— ▼ ——————

Nikki and Ian went back through the door, leaving Tiggy to close it behind them. Nikki jumped when he heard the whoosh of the door being closed and sealed.

"I sure hope that she can keep opening and closing that door, or else we might very well become a part of this ancient wonder."

"As long as she has that piece, she should be able to get us out," said Ian, holding the lantern high.

"Should?" cried Nikki, turning around.

"Here, hold up your lantern and stop worrying about getting out. I was just scaring you anyway."

"Not very funny, Ian. Tiggy already just about scared the life out of me."

They continued walking downward until they came to what appeared to be a corridor.

"What are we looking for in here?" asked Nikki.

"I imagine that we are looking for the pharaoh's crook. All Tiggy said was that the lotus flower would show the way. So far, I haven't seen anything to show us the way."

"Maybe not, but look at this," said Nikki, holding the lantern next to a statue of Hathor. "Here is a lotus flower and an inscription. I can't read it very well. Blast it! I wish I would have studied those hieroglyphics better when Tiggy asked me to on the boat trip over here."

"Can you make out any of the words? Even just a few words might help."

"Well, one says 'beware' and this one says 'way.' So maybe we are on the right track," Nikki replied hopefully.

"Let's keep going," said Ian, gesturing with his lantern.

They continued down the corridor for several minutes until they ran into a dead end.

Which way do we go? wondered Ian.

"Tiggy always says to start off on the right foot, so I say let's go to the right."

"Right it is then."

Not fifteen yards down the corridor, they ran into another dead end.

"Well, this wasn't the right way," said Nikki.

"Yes, it was," responded Ian. "Look at the wall; the lotus flower is in the dead center of that hieroglyphic seal. I wonder what we do now."

"I think we need to go back and get Tiggy. She would know exactly what all this stuff means," replied Nikki, waving his hand toward the wall.

"That's true, but then who would hold the door open while she goes and looks for the other clues?"

"Maybe there is a key on the inside. If I were that sneaky high priest, I wouldn't have left a door wide open for everyone to see my secret passageway."

"True. I never thought about that," said Ian, shaking his head.

"Come on," said Nikki, turning back toward the corridor. "Let's go back and get her."

"I agree," replied Ian. "I wasn't comfortable with leaving her there by herself anyway."

Retracing their steps, they arrived back at the stone door, the return trip taking much less time than the outbound trip.

"Look around, Nikki, and see if you can find that lotus symbol. It has to be the key that opens the door from the inside."

Nikki and Ian searched everywhere for a symbol of the lotus flower.

Frustrated, Nikki sat down on the floor. "It has to be around here somewhere. Hapuseneb wouldn't have been stupid enough not to have another way to open that door. It just has to be around here somewhere," he said again as he picked up a piece of stone and threw it at the wall in frustration.

A sliding sound was heard as a small section of the wall opened to reveal the shape of the lotus.

"You did it, Nikki!" shouted Ian, jumping to his feet. "Now all we have to do is wait for Tiggy to open the door."

No sooner were the words out of Ian's mouth than the door began to open. Both rushed out with the intent to bring her back as fast as possible.

"Tiggy, come quickly! You have to come with us."

"What are you shouting about, Nikki? Did you find the second clue?" she asked.

"No, we didn't, but we did find out where to begin looking for it," he replied.

"Then why didn't you get the clue?" she asked with confusion.

"Why?" answered Ian. "Because we can't read the hieroglyphics."

Nikki turned around and pretended to tie his shoelace, avoiding her eyes.

"Well, I see that I'll have to give you two a crash course on reading them."

"Let's go!" said Nikki, pulling on her arm. "It's getting late, and we don't know what we are going to find down there."

"Nikki, I can't go, because I have to open the door," Tiggy said.

"Oh no, you don't," beamed Nikki proudly. "I found a keyhole, so to speak, on the inside of the passageway. Pull the lotus off, and we'll make a run for it."

"I'm for trying," said Tiggy. "Everybody have their stuff, just in case?"

"Tiggy, are you sure about this?" questioned Ian before they started off.

"I'm as sure as I can possibly be," she said while shrugging her shoulders.

She placed the lotus flower into the piece on the stone column as Nikki and Ian went through the door. Pulling the lotus off, she raced toward the opening. She made it through with time to spare. As the door closed, she felt a gentle breeze swirl around them. She could faintly hear a soft voice saying, "Come … follow me."

"Show us the way," she said aloud.

Ian and Nikki turned around and gave her a curious glance but said nothing. Down the spiral staircase they went. Their lanterns looked like fireflies dancing in the moonlight. Coming upon the corridor, they turned to the right, following the path that Ian and Nikki had taken earlier.

"Come," whispered the gentle voice, as if leading them to the location.

"Did you hear something, Ian?" asked Nikki.

"Yes, I did."

"Good. I thought that maybe I was beginning to hear things."

Tiggy, out in front, quickly followed the breeze that continued to dance around her. Turning again to the right, they soon saw the huge wall relief.

"See the flower in the middle?" asked Nikki.

"Yes, I see it. It appears to be the same size as the one in my hand," she responded while comparing it to the piece she now held.

"Well, what are we waiting for? Place it on the wall," said Ian.

"Not so fast. We have to be careful," replied Tiggy. "Hapuseneb was no fool. He wouldn't set this symbol in such a visible place where anyone who found this piece could quickly get to the next clue."

Tiggy handed the piece to Nikki and said, "Hold on to that while I take a closer look." Stepping toward the wall, she began to read the hieroglyphics, looking for clues. Moments later, she stepped back. "Just as I thought. There is a subtle warning for those claiming to know the value of the lotus. Listen: 'It is worthy of the daughter of Amun-Ra, Khnumetamun Hatshepsut. Only those who truly believed her to be the pharaoh of Upper and Lower Egypt will find what they seek.'" Tiggy paused, glancing at the other inscriptions.

Turning around, she said, "Well, there is no doubt in my mind that she truly was the pharaoh. She inherited that right from her father, and Tuthmosis III probably murdered her in order to gain the throne."

"Without a doubt," agreed Ian. "From everything that you have said, Tuthmosis III seems to definitely be a bad character. He probably hated the fact that she, being a woman, was successful as a ruler."

"Very successful," added Nikki. "I know that her treasure must be immense."

"Well, even if it's not, I would like to have more proof about her reign and her everyday life," Tiggy said. "To touch the things she touched and to wear the jewels she wore. In a way, she would live on, despite the fact that Tuthmosis III maliciously destroyed all the information pertaining to her."

"You believe," whispered the wind. "This is both good and bad. Come quickly and I will explain."

"How?" responded Tiggy.

"Place the lotus and prepare," went on the voice in the wind.

"Prepare for what?" she questioned.

"Did you hear that?" Nikki asked Ian.

"Yes, I heard a woman's voice talking through the wind."

Turning around, Tiggy asked, "Should we do this or not?"

"Well ..." they began.

But before they could fully respond, Tiggy cried out as the hand that held the lotus piece was pulled toward the lotus carving on the wall. As she fell against the wall, the piece fitted perfectly. The ground began to tremble violently. She screamed as the ground beneath her gave way, and she began to fall.

"Ian! Nikki!" she screamed as she fell.

They both jumped to catch her before she fell, but they were not quick enough, and downward she plummeted.

They could hear her scream grow fainter as the lantern light disappeared from their view. Both knelt in the sand, each feeling that Tiggy could not have survived the fall.

Nikki leaned over and screamed her name again and again in despair.

Minutes ticked by as neither said a word, each stunned.

Sitting back on the sand, Nikki, unashamed, began to cry. Ian sat back on his heels, determined not to give way to his grief. He decided that he must at least go and retrieve her body. He would not leave her to lie in some ancient temple. Getting to his feet, he retrieved some rope and poured more oil into his lantern.

Nikki glanced up and asked, "What are you doing?"

Without looking at Nikki, he pulled the rope out and quietly said, "I'm going to get her."

Nikki nodded his head. "I'll go too."

Ian tied the rope around a nearby statue and threw it into the hole in the ground. Nikki, bending over the hole, suddenly hushed Ian.

"Shh … be still. I hear something."

Throwing the rope down, Ian rushed over and lay on the ground.

"Tiggy! Tiggy, can you hear us?" All was silent. Again they cried out, "Tiggy! Answer us if you can."

"Yes," came a faint reply.

Jubilant, they both shouted, "Hold on! We're coming!"

"Shine the light in the hole before you come," replied Tiggy. "There's a drop, and then you land on a slide of sorts. Watch the landing; it's a real doozy."

Ian and Nikki were so relieved to hear her voice that they began laughing with joy.

"Come on, Nikki," Ian said. "Get your bag. I'll untie this rope and take it with us. We might need it later. This place is full of surprises."

"I agree," said Nikki as he held his lantern down into the hole. "Look! I see the slide that she is talking about. It looks as if it is made out of marble or some kind of igneous rock."

"Hey, you two, I don't mean to be pushy, but my lantern went out, and I am down here in the dark with some creepy-crawly thing moving around in the sand."

"Hold on. I'm coming," said Nikki, jumping down through the hole and onto the slide.

Down he went with a scream of delight. "Maybe that vizier wasn't such a stick in the mud after all. That was fun," he said after he reached the bottom, landing on top of Tiggy.

"Get off me, Nikki. You're heavy," she complained, pushing him away.

"Sorry."

Holding the lantern high, they glanced around at their surroundings for the first time.

"Whew! What's that smell?" said Nikki, fanning the air.

"It's the air. It's stale. I bet that no one has entered this chamber for the last thousand or so years."

"Then the last ones here must have been pretty smelly to leave such an awful stink behind."

Tiggy laughed and then told Nikki to grab the torch from the wall and light it with the lantern. Hollering upward, she called for Ian to hurry.

Quickly he came sliding down the ramp, landing in the sand just as Nikki and Tiggy had done.

"Pretty handy little idea," Ian said, "but I must say that it scared the life out of me when I thought you fell all the way down here. I am glad that you are all right."

"Thank you," replied Tiggy with a smile. "So am I. Now, let's get looking for the next clue, the crook."

Hours passed while the three intently searched the chamber for the pharaoh's crook. Tiggy began reading the walls, while Ian and Nikki dug in the sand at the base of the walls. Ian went so far as to try to see if anything was carved on the ceiling by trying to stand upon the slide time and time again. Tiredness and frustration were beginning to take their toll. Each was looking more and more tired. Finally, Tiggy glanced one more time at her watch and declared that it was time to quit.

"I think we're finished for today," she stated while brushing sand off her pants.

"Yes," agreed Ian, "this is getting us nowhere. We'll be refreshed and ready to start again in the morning."

"I agree too," chimed in Nikki. "I could use some fresh air."

Packing up their canvas bags, they decided to head back up the slide and call it a day. It took them almost forty-five minutes to retrace their steps out to the temple ramp.

Looking out over the sands of the desert toward the setting sun, they could feel a sense of accomplishment for a hard day's work. A sudden breeze swirled around them, and the tender voice was heard to say, "You have done well. We will meet by the next setting of the sun."

Slowly, as if to savor the last few minutes of the sunset, they walked down the last ramp toward the camp.

CHAPTER SIX

▼

An hour after sunrise, Ian and Nikki emerged from their tents. They sat in front of the fire, watching their breakfast cook in the skillet and planning out the day. They agreed that finding the second clue had not been as easy as they had anticipated.

"I feel that the closer we come to finding the auta, the more dangerous it is going to become," declared Ian.

"Definitely," agreed Nikki. "We had a warning already," he continued while flinging a handful of dates into his mouth.

"When?"

"Before you came, the wind warned us that only the bravest would survive."

"Hmm ... somehow that part was left out of the telling."

"What was left out?" Tiggy asked Ian as she sat down beside him.

Startled, he turned and said, "Good morning! Sleep well?"

"Yes, I did. Not one single vision, thankfully. Now, what were you two discussing?"

"The warning to be brave," interjected Nikki.

"Oh yes, that. I forgot to mention it, probably because to be involved in any part of this adventure, you need to be brave. That's a given."

Both nodded in agreement while they began eating their breakfast.

Half past nine in the morning, they arrived back at the gaping hole in the underground corridor. Tiggy and Nikki took turns sliding downward into the chamber. While Nikki relit the torches, Tiggy unpacked additional lanterns, hoping to provide more light to aid their search.

"Much better," said Ian after he slid down into the chamber.

"What are you doing with the rope?" asked Nikki while replacing a lit torch to its holder.

"Oh, that's to make it easier for us to get out of here, kind of like a railing to hold on to while we climb back up," Ian said.

"Good idea," agreed Tiggy. "It was tough going up yesterday."

Ian pulled the rope taut and then bent down to tie it to a protruding stone at the base of the slide.

Tiggy set a lantern down next to him, and he gasped.

"Oh my gosh!"

"What?" both Tiggy and Nikki said, turning around to look at him.

"Look!" he said, pointing to the stone he had tied the rope around. "The pharaoh's crook!"

"What!" they said in unison as they rushed toward him.

"That's it! That's it!" they cried in delight.

"Touch it and pull it out!" stated Tiggy.

Ian placed his hand on the stone and tried to pull it out as he had seen Tiggy do with the lotus. But nothing happened. He tried again but still was not successful. Puzzled, he sat down in the sand. "I don't understand."

"Maybe it's not the one," stated Nikki, looking over at Tiggy.

She just shrugged while turning away from Nikki as he went to try. Then suddenly she felt a shove to her back.

"Don't push!" she shouted as she stumbled forward.

"I didn't push you," said Nikki standing up.

"You didn't, but someone did."

The wind that they had become accustomed to swirled around her and demanded, "You must pull the pharaoh's crook."

Tiggy looked at Ian and Nikki and raised her eyebrows. "Should I?"

"Why not?" responded Ian. "You were able to pull the lotus from the statue."

Kneeling in the sand, Tiggy extended her hands to touch the crook. The lotus grew warm within her shirt, as if calling to the crook.

As before, the cool, dark surface of the rock turned warm and golden under her touch. She could feel it changing form and gradually falling away from its surroundings. At last, it was loose enough to pull free.

She stood up, admiring its beauty. It was roughly the same size as the lotus. Like the lotus, the crook was raised from the gold in a high relief design and made of pure gold too. However, it was banded with inlaid stones— sapphires, it appeared at first glance—and stripes of heavy gold. And again the corners and sides had strange rounded pieces of gold sticking out in a random design, much like the edges of a puzzle piece.

"Wow! Would you look at that!" exclaimed Ian.

"It's beautiful," said Tiggy.

"It's the next clue," declared Nikki, pointing to its end. "See? It's rounded, and I just bet that it fits into the lotus piece."

Tiggy reached into her blouse and pulled out a pouch that hung around her neck on a string. Opening it up, she took out the lotus piece and joined it with the pharaoh's crook. When the two pieces touched, out poured a brilliant golden light; they heard the sound of rumbling as the stones began to move.

"Uh-oh," said Nikki, staring over her shoulder.

Ian and Tiggy slowly turned as the side of the slide opened to reveal yet another hidden passageway.

"Hand me that torch, Nikki," asked Ian as he walked toward the opening. Nikki did as he was told and quickly brought him the torch. Leaning in, Ian saw that it was another corridor.

"Come on! Grab those lanterns and let's go."

"Bring everything," said Tiggy as she placed the two pieces into the pouch.

They quickly repacked what they had taken out and stepped into the new corridor.

"What are we looking for, the auta?" asked Ian. "So maybe that's the next clue."

"Scarab," the wind whispered.

"Scarab?" Tiggy asked as she glanced around, trying to find the wind.

"Scarab," the voice repeated faintly as the wind moved down the wide stone corridor.

Lighting torches they found along their way, they arrived at a large door some five minutes later. In place of a handle was a scarab. Without hesitating, Tiggy reached out and touched it; just as before, it changed and came away transformed into a beautiful golden piece in her hand. Pulling out the other two pieces, she placed them on the sand.

"What are you doing?" Ian inquired as he knelt beside her.

"Look—these are like puzzle pieces," she began as she placed the pieces beside each other. "They each have ends and sides that are rounded. I placed the lotus and the pharaoh's crook together to open this passage," she said while connecting the two pieces.

"Looking at the scarab, you can see that it fits into the bottom of the crook," said Nikki, pointing, as he squatted down beside her in sand.

"Exactly!" replied Tiggy.

"But where will it take us if we put the scarab into the puzzle?" asked Ian.

"Good question, and the only problem is, I've no idea."

Turning the scarab piece over in her hand, she noticed for the first time tiny hieroglyphics etched into its back.

"I didn't notice these," she said, pointing to them.

Nikki quickly turned the other two pieces over to examine them as well.

"There are only a few etched on the lotus," she said.

"There are more on the crook," Nikki said, pointing toward the bottom.

"Yes, there are!" she exclaimed.

Nikki handed Tiggy the crook, and they waited while she removed the lotus and then joined the scarab to the crook.

"I cannot read it," she said with evident disappointment. "It is too small. What I need is a magnifying lens," she said as she passed the pieces to Ian.

"Far too small," Ian said. "It's amazing that they were able to engrave anything so tiny."

"They had the ability to do so much more than we know," said Tiggy, standing up. "Well," she said, drawing in a deep breath, "are we ready to put all the pieces together?"

"Ready as we'll ever be," stated Ian.

"Ready," said Nikki as she glanced his way.

Tiggy joined the pieces one by one and watched as the large door swung open before them. The stagnant air poured forth, causing them to draw back, as a wind rushed past them.

Ian bravely took the first step, placing the flaming torch before him. Nikki followed, standing beside him and holding a lantern aloft. Tiggy brought up the rear, bringing even more light into the chamber.

Moments passed as each stood still, awestruck. They stood in a square room that was completely decorated with hieroglyphics and depictions of various scenes. Six large stone columns supported the ceiling, each not only carved but also gilded with gold and encrusted with semiprecious stones. Several steps led down to a sunken floor and something was in the center of the room. It was too dim to make out anything other than what appeared to be a table. Walking around the elevated edge of the room, Tiggy passed several cartouches bearing the name of Queen Hatshepsut on her way to light the wall torches she knew instinctively would be there.

"Light the torches," she said. "I think we've done it!"

The room came more into view as Ian began lighting the torches on the opposite side of the room. Tiggy could now make out a beautifully carved table, and upon it sat an ornate gold chest. She began to walk toward it when Nikki's question stopped her.

He said, "Why does the floor seem to be moving? Is it water?"

"What do you mean the floor is moving?" questioned Ian. "I can't believe there would be water in here. I don't hear a thing that even sounds like moving water."

"It seems like the floor is moving," was all Nikki repeated.

"Floors don't move," said Tiggy as she stopped beside him.

Both Ian and Tiggy glanced at the floor and saw what Nikki meant.

Tiggy's eyes grew wide as Ian threw his torch onto the floor in the center of the room. She let out a gasp as she saw hundreds of snakes slithering over each other.

"There had to be snakes! I knew it couldn't be this easy," she cried out, stepping backward.

"Uh, Tiggy," said Nikki calmly, "maybe because the auta is a snake, and they guard the sacred piece."

"Yes, I know," she moaned. "But of all the things, real snakes! And after all these centuries, they still guard the piece?"

Ian shook his head in dismay. "I don't mind a few snakes, but this is too much even for me," he declared, coming over to stand by her.

"No big deal," stated Nikki. "I love snakes. This doesn't really bother me at all," he stated, trying to sound brave.

"Good! Then you go get the chest!" she declared.

"I would, but it would be a waste of time. You've been the only one, so far, who's been able to get the pieces and open the doors," he responded with a shrug.

"There's no way I'm going to walk through hundreds of snakes! You must be crazy! This adventure just ended right here and now!" she retorted, turning on her heel and heading back out the door.

"No!" said the wind as it rushed at her.

"Yes!" Tiggy declared. "I hate snakes! I won't do this!"

"Only the bravest!" pleaded the wind. "You must come; the hour draws nearer."

Tiggy closed her eyes tightly and could see, in her mind's eye, the young woman's eyes. The eyes begged her to try, and Tiggy knew she had to face her fears in order to save this woman from hers.

Drawing a deep breath, Tiggy quietly turned and said, "I'll do it!"

Nikki and Ian were shocked. Neither expected her to ever walk through snakes for anything, especially for some voice they heard in the wind.

"Hand me a torch please!" she said, steeling herself for her first step. While Ian brought the torch, she bent down to tuck her pant legs into her boots, hoping that would lessen the chance of a snake crawling up her pants. She took the torch from Ian's hand, closed her eyes, and stepped into the snakes, heading for the chest.

Tiggy took the torch and waved it before her feet, causing the snakes to slither away from the intense heat. "Ooh, yuck," she said as one hissed at her. "I hate this. I really, really hate this." Ian and Nikki watched in amazement as she waved the torch and kicked snakes out of the way with her boots.

Finally, she reached the table that contained the chest. Holding the torch in one hand, she attempted to pick the chest up and move it. However, it was too heavy for her to move without help.

"One of you come over here please and help me lift the chest out from around these snakes," she asked as she continued to wave the torch around her feet.

"I'll go," said Nikki. "Ian, you follow me and make a path with those torches from the walls. That will make it easier for us to carry this out without worrying about the snakes."

A shimmer caught Tiggy's eye as she went to move the chest with Nikki. "Wait ... what's this?" She bent down and saw a long, thick gold chain hanging around the base of the chest. It was a large disk with narrow strips of thick gold shooting outward from the center that was representative of the sun. The golden rays shot out from it, making it quite brilliant in the torchlight. Sensing that the chain was indeed important, as it had been put in a place of importance around the base of the chest, she quickly put it over her head. Immediately she dropped the torch to the ground and clutched her forehead. She screamed out at the pain that surged through her. She staggered and fell against the table, causing it to rock.

"What is it?" asked Nikki, grabbing on to her shoulder.

Tiggy opened her eyes and saw the beautiful woman standing before her. "You must open the chest and get the auta. Time is drawing near for me."

"Is there a curse upon the chest?" Tiggy asked. "Can we move it without being harmed?"

"There is no curse for *you* opening the chest," she emphasized, "only for those who do not believe that Hatshepsut is the rightful pharaoh."

"Why must we hurry?" asked Tiggy of the woman. "It has been hidden all these thousands of years. Surely it will come to no harm now."

"I will answer all your questions when you come, but for now, go and open the chest."

Can I trust you? Tiggy thought.

"Yes," replied a voice that she heard even through the ache that now pulsated through her forehead.

Ian was shaking her when she opened her eyes. Confused, she asked, "How did I get over here by the door to the passageway? Where's the chest?"

"The chest is fine," he said anxiously as he knelt next to her. "More importantly, how are you?"

"I'm fine."

"You know, I rushed over and got you before any of the snakes had a chance to crawl on you."

"I thank you for that!" she said while sitting up and rubbing her forehead.

"Another vision?" asked Nikki as he handed her some water.

"Yes. I don't know why they have to be so painful. When they come, it's almost as if I am not here anymore, like I'm transported through time. I see everything perfectly as if I am really there."

"What did you see this time?" inquired Ian. He noticed that the three-inch scab with its oblong shape on her forehead seemed to be more pronounced than usual.

"I saw the same young woman that I've seen since the beginning. She keeps telling me to come because her time is drawing near."

"Near to what?" asked Nikki.

"I have no idea. She told me to open the chest and get the auta. At least we know that the auta is in the chest," she said, trying to sound positive.

"Well, let's open it," replied Nikki.

"Let's read the inscription before we do anything," said Tiggy, pointing to the top of the chest as she began to read aloud. "'By sacred law a journey awaits those who open this chest. Seek ye the royal robes. Only the pure in heart will accomplish the journey that they seek. Beware, the fairest that comes, of the warrior of the second son of Amun-Ra, for there is evil in his heart. Have courage, o mighty warriors, for whom ye protect. The reward will be great for those that have the strength to do what is just.'"

"Curious, isn't it?" said Ian. "I wonder what's meant by 'a journey.'"

"Maybe the journey that we'll take will be the one to find the treasure," suggested Nikki.

Turning, Tiggy glanced at them and said, "Do we open the chest and get the auta?"

"That's what we came for, so let's open her up," supplied Nikki.

Ian nodded his agreement, and Tiggy bent to open the lid of the chest. Slowly she pushed the lid back to view the piece that had inspired the journey. It lay on a bed of golden silk, still beautiful despite the intervening centuries, untouched by time. The piece itself was similar to the other three pieces that they had already acquired. It too was made of solid gold, with the auta raised and encrusted with jewels. It was made in the typical cobra design seen on the crown of all pharaohs and was roughly three to four inches long. Turning it over, Tiggy could discern the same tiny hieroglyphics that were on the other pieces.

"It's as beautiful as the others," Tiggy said. "I just can't believe the marvelous workmanship that this has. I wonder how all that skill could've been lost through the ages. It's so very beautiful." She handed it to Ian.

"Are we going to join it with the other pieces or wait until later?" he said while handing it to Nikki.

"I think we have to join them together in order to receive the next clue. It's obvious that there are more pieces to this puzzle yet undiscovered," replied Tiggy as she drew from inside her shirt the small pouch that held the other three pieces. The pieces all together weighed only a little over a half of a pound, and Tiggy had felt it necessary to wear them at all times so that they would not become lost or misplaced.

Sitting on the sand in the doorway to the room that held the chest, she began to join the pieces; she reached up toward Nikki, and he placed the auta into her hand. The sun amulet, which she had placed around her neck, began to glow with a golden light.

"Look at your necklace," said Ian.

Tiggy placed the auta into the puzzle that she held in her hand, and suddenly a brilliant light poured forth from everywhere—the walls, the ceiling, and the floors of the room. The light was so bright, in fact, that it caused them to close their eyes against it. A great noise like a loud crack of thunder was heard, and the sand started to shift and swirl violently around them.

"Tiggy, what's happening?" yelled Nikki.

"Ian! Nikki!" Tiggy screamed above it all.

"I don't know. Just hold on to one another," she hollered back.

"You're slipping! Hold on tighter, Tiggy!" shouted Ian.

"I can't! My hands are stuck to the pieces."

"Nikki, grab her other arm!"

"I've got it! How much longer?" yelled Nikki over the violent swirling of the sand.

As the three struggled to hold on to one another, the wind pulled and pushed their bodies with terrific force. Then, as if tired of trying to destroy them, it finally began to calm. Several seconds passed before a shaky and scared voice was heard.

CHAPTER SEVEN

▼

The sand slowed to a stop, and Tiggy opened her eyes; before her stood the woman that she had seen so often.

"Is this another vision?" she questioned of her.

The woman smiled as she reached her hand out to help Tiggy to her feet.

"You have done well to find the pieces, and you had the courage to face your fears."

At her words, Ian and Nikki opened their eyes.

"What on earth!" said Ian, looking around the room that was now free of the sand and dust of the ages, a room that resembled the one that they were in only moments before yet now shone with golden splendor.

"Where are we, and where are all the snakes?" asked Nikki as he stood up, startled. Shaking the sand off, he asked, "Who are you?"

Turning, Tiggy glanced from Ian to Nikki in amazement. "You're here. How can this be? You have never been in one of these visions."

"Well, we're here and she is too," sputtered out Nikki, still somewhat dazed.

"I can't believe this," muttered Ian, rising to his feet.

The woman, seeing their bewildered expressions, said, "This is not a dream."

Tiggy watched her closely, realizing that what she was seeing was more than a vision; it was, in fact, very real. "May I ask who you are? You never once told me your name."

"I am the youngest daughter of Pharaoh Hatshepsut, Princess Merira Hatshepsut."

Tiggy's eyes grew wide. "What is your calendar year?"

"The end of the reign of Pharaoh Hatshepsut," she finished sadly.

"Your mother, I mean the pharaoh, has disappeared, correct?" Tiggy questioned.

"You speak the truth. I wish that it was not so, but, alas, it has happened."

"Have you been approached for your hand in marriage?" she continued to question.

"You again are correct. That is why I needed you to come quickly. My time was drawing near, and I must protect what has been my mother's," she stated as she paced back and forth in front of them.

Nikki, not quite sure she was real, reached out and poked the princess on the arm.

Startled, Princess Merira stopped and stared.

"Sorry," he explained to Tiggy. "I just wanted to make sure she was real."

Tiggy quickly explained that Nikki meant no disrespect and that he was trying to see if she was in fact a real person and not a dream.

Nodding her head in understanding, the princess continued her story. "My mother spoke of you; she told me that a fair one would be sent. She saw you in a dream and discussed with me what I must do if anything were to happen to her. That was many seasons ago. I have patiently waited for your arrival. I must say, though, you dress strangely. I was foretold that you are from a distant land, but even I did not expect a woman to dress in such clothing," she said as she tentatively reached out and touched Tiggy's pant leg and shirt.

Tiggy laughed and said, "We have come from a distant time, but not a distant land. We were standing in this very room when I placed the pieces together. However, we were not in the year 1458 BC or the end of the reign of Pharaoh Hatshepsut."

The princess looked confused and said, "A distant time? Of this it was not foretold."

At this point Ian interrupted, completely stunned by what was occurring. "Are you telling me that we are now, currently, at this very moment, in the year 1458? BC? That somehow we've traveled back in time by joining those gold pieces together?"

Not understanding what he had asked, Princess Merira turned to Tiggy for her to translate.

"You are correct, Magi," replied the princess, not worried in the least when Tiggy told her what Ian had asked.

"Uh, Your Highness, I'm Ian, her friend."

Again Tiggy translated for Ian, thoroughly wishing that both Nikki and Ian had learned the language months ago when she had asked them to.

The princess spoke again, "This is not a dream. You must believe what your eyes are telling you. And as her warriors, by the law, you had to come to protect her, it has been written, it is sacred."

"Uh, excuse me, Princess," interjected Nikki as Tiggy translated yet again. "I'm not a warrior."

"Those who come with her protect her; they are warriors," corrected the princess. "If you are with this woman, then you are her magi, warriors for the royal family. But speaking of the magi, we must retire to my rooms and change your clothes into attire fitting of your stations. Here—put this around you, and hide what you do not need to take," she said, handing each of them a length of cloth. "We can always come later and retrieve the items that you need. Come quickly; we need to get away from here, because Hessam, the head magi to Pharaoh Tuthmosis III, is very suspicious of me and follows me everywhere."

"Is that because you're soon to be the God Wife of the pharaoh?" asked Tiggy as she rolled up her pants and wrapped the cloth around her.

"Yes, and keep quiet, for your voice will give you away before time. Come quickly."

It was hard for them not to look around at the grandeur of it all. The walls were beautifully decorated with carvings and paintings of the different gods and goddesses worshipped in ancient Egypt, ducks flying over the Nile River, soldiers hunting wild animals, men harvesting their crops—a myriad of scenes, all colored and in their original hand-painted state, untouched by the ravages of time. The wonder continued as they walked through the magnificent halls, seeing sentries on duty, slaves hauling food and wine, serving girls carrying spice-scented oils and flowery perfumes, and some bearing urns full of tall, strange-looking white flowers.

The princess pointed out several different corridors and explained where they led, but she did so too quickly for the trio to remember all the details. Passing her own personal sentries, who wore black and gold cloth and carried curved, wicked-looking swords, she immediately dismissed her handmaidens and male slaves with a clap and wave of her hands. Looking around, she cautiously told Tiggy, Ian, and Nikki to remove the cloth that covered their clothing.

"This place is great, Tiggy!" Nikki cried out, unable to contain his excitement. "Did you see those guards with those massive swords? This is something that my father is never going to believe!"

"You're right," Tiggy replied. "Never in my life could I imagine anything such as this." Tiggy spun around slowly, taking in the room.

"I can't believe any of this is real," said Ian. "I feel as if I have fallen asleep and this is all a dream."

"If this is a dream, it's the most original one I've ever had," responded Nikki as he eyed a large fruit bowl.

The princess, noticing his gaze, said graciously, "You are hungry? Then you must eat; all of you must eat. Once you have eaten, I will hide you until I can create a plan to bring you into the city without suspicion."

"Why are we here?" asked Tiggy as she bit into a delicious date.

The princess walked around the room, picking up various items. Finally, she paused. "I have no choice but to wed Tuthmosis III; it has been decreed, and I could lose my life if I fail in my royal obligation. I do not mind being the God Wife, for it holds more power than a mere princess. However, I do not want the wealth of my mother to be stolen and erased from history by thieves, whether royal or common."

She looked at her audience; seeing their interest, she continued. "Please be comfortable," she said, waving toward cushions on the floor. "My mother was a great pharaoh and did many wonderful things for this land. She had a dream that foretold of a fair stranger coming from the west to save her wealth from the greed of those now in power. She desperately wanted to hide it from all who would choose to use it poorly. She commanded her royal vizier and high priest to hide it for her before she disappeared."

"That would be Hapuseneb," interjected Tiggy.

"You are well informed for someone from a distant time."

"I've thoroughly studied what we call ancient Egyptian culture and life," she replied.

"Good, for it will serve you well while you are here."

"Tiggy, ask the princess if we are going to be here for a long time," asked Ian respectfully toward the princess.

"Just as long as it is necessary; then you will return. And please, call me Merira or Hatshepsut, whichever you prefer, for I know you mean no disrespect to my royal title. The time from which you come has pharaohs?"

"Not in America, where I come from, but there is a queen in the country of England, where Ian and Nikki come from," said Tiggy.

"These lands ... are they more powerful than Egypt?"

"Yes, much more powerful, Princess, I mean Merira," finished Tiggy as she glanced at Ian and Nikki, wondering if she had said too much.

Nodding, she said, "This is interesting. We will talk more when you are not in so much danger."

"Danger?" said Nikki, grasping at a word he did know. "I thought that we would be safe here with the princess, Tiggy."

"Yes, according to Merira we are in danger from Hessam, the head magi, for if he finds us he will surely try to kill us."

"Why?" asked Ian. "We are no threat to the rule of Tuthmosis III."

"No, not directly, but according to Merira, we are still a threat to the wealth that he covets."

Sitting down on some elegant silk cushions in front of them, the princess adjusted her garments and began again. "You see, my mother was overheard in the telling of her dream to me. Tuthmosis knows that one will come seeking the final pieces that unlock the key to my mother's treasure. No one will be able to find and use the key except the one who was foretold to in the dream." Eyeing Tiggy, Merira said, "That is you!"

"Why me, Merira?" Tiggy asked. "I have no special meaning to your mother or to Egypt, for that matter."

"It does not matter; you have been chosen, and you must fulfill what is your destiny," the princess retorted. "But for now, you must hide. I will have my most trusted handmaiden take you from the city and disguise you. Then you must come back and find the key."

Rapidly Merira unfolded a plan that would allow Tiggy, Ian, and Nikki to wander around the palace and city unhindered. "You must never be without your veil," she admonished Tiggy while covering her hair, "for your light hair will give you away immediately."

"I understand, Your Highness. I will do my best to keep it covered for all of our sakes."

Early the next morning, Tiggy, Nikki, and Ian entered the great city of Thebes. Fascinated, they watched the city come to life in the early dawn: vendors putting out their fruits and vegetables, others putting out their trinkets and cloth, a few people walking toward the marketplace to purchase needed items. In the distance, they saw men with suntanned backs heading into the fields behind oxen or camels. To their twenty-first-century eyes, these sights held all the wonder and allure of a mysterious ancient time. They feasted their eyes upon scenes that up to this time had been confined to their imaginations. This was truly the Egypt that history had forgotten, ordinary yet unique to those who have never seen the likes of it before.

Tiggy was becoming nervous to the point of agitation as they neared the great entrance to the palace of Deir-el-Bahari.

The old woman, who was small and bent, with eyes full of wisdom, and who had been with the princess since birth, sensed her fear. Reaching her hand across Ian, she patted her cheek, saying, "All will go well. Do what comes natural to you. I see that you have an ability and presence to lead; do so, and it will serve you well this day. Remember, the pharaoh likes a beautiful woman."

They were greeted at the palace ramp by Merira and many royal officials. Holding out her arms, Princess Merira greeted Tiggy with an enormous show of affection.

"Greetings, fair Princess Amanda. I trust your journey to us was uneventful."

Tiggy returned the affectionate hug. "Yes, Princess Merira, it was uneventful, yet it was exciting to actually see the powerful kingdom that is spoken of with great awe throughout the world. Again, Ra bless you for your gracious invitation."

Clapping her hands together, Princess Merira demanded, "Quickly, show the magi to her room. Come—let us adjourn to the throne room." Throwing a meaningful glance at Tiggy, she said more softly, "You will be granted an audience with Tuthmosis III." Linking her arm through Tiggy's, she waved Ian and Nikki to follow the others. Tiggy nodded her head slightly. Leaning in close to Tiggy, the princess cautiously asked, "From what kingdom do you come?"

"I come from Rome; it is presently small but will one day rule Egypt for a time. I met you many years ago when we were both small. We spent only one day together until I fell ill; at that time, you invited me to one day return."

"This is good; you are very quick to invent such a story in such a short amount of time."

"Let us just hope that the pharaoh does not see through this whole story," began Tiggy as she glanced around the beautiful halls of the palace. Tiggy was amazed as she compared the present immaculate condition of the palace to its crumbling appearance in her own time. It saddened her to think that the world would miss so much because of robbers and the looting of invading armies. She sighed loudly as she looked around and thought of what was to come for this beautiful palace.

Hearing her sigh, Merira whispered, "What is wrong?"

"Oh, it's nothing. I was just marveling at the beauty I see here and comparing it to the ruins I've seen in my own time."

"Ruins?" exclaimed the princess with shock.

"Yes," responded Tiggy sadly. "This palace is nothing like this in my own time. It has been looted and is in great disrepair. The gardens no longer exist; in fact, very little is left except the main structure, and it's been disfigured by time and by the armies that will invade Egypt in the years to come. All of the treasures are gone, and there's not much known about your mother and very little about you, except your name and that you became Tuthmosis III's wife."

Princess Merira looked upon Tiggy with shock and horror. "This cannot be true! How could all of this have happened?"

"It is a long story, spanning thousands of years. However, my friends and I are most fortunate to have witnessed what no eye has seen for hundreds of decades—to touch and to hear and to see what has not been written of or seen in many years."

"But we must live on," declared the princess.

"You will live on, but very little will be known. We're determined to learn all that we can about the life and people of this time. We'll try to find your mother's hidden wealth, thus shedding some light on your people and your culture. That's our desire anyway," she finished.

"You are truly the chosen one to save what has been my mother's and my country's greatest possessions. I know in my spirit that I can entrust them to you for safekeeping," responded the princess as she grasped Tiggy's hand tightly.

Turning left, Tiggy could now see that the golden corridor led to a great room flanked by two large columns. She assumed correctly as they entered it, moments later, that it was the throne room of Pharaoh Tuthmosis III.

Tiggy was not impressed with the pharaoh, for his eyes seemed not to have the depth of character one expected to see in a ruler of such a great land. He was slightly taller than Tiggy and was young, as she had expected. His angular face had pleasant features with high cheekbones typical of most Egyptians. His set jaw, however, announced that he would brook no opposition from anyone. She also sensed, at once, that he had a roving eye for any new female entering his court. Even as he extended his hand in greeting to Princess Merira, his eyes were on Tiggy.

Chapter Eight

▼

"Greetings to you, my lovely Princess Merira. What tidings do you bring to me this day?" Tuthmosis III said while grasping her fingers within his and pulling her up to stand beside him, leaving Tiggy to stand alone by herself in front of him.

"Today, gracious Pharaoh, I bring to you Her Royal Highness Amanda from Rome, the beautiful city across the great sea."

At her words, Tiggy did the only thing she knew to do, which was to curtsy to the ground as she did before the queen of England at Buckingham Palace. She stayed in that position with her eyes to the ground until the pharaoh astonished both Tiggy and Merira by rising from his throne.

The pharaoh stood in front of Tiggy, intrigued at the posture of servitude from a royal personage. Stretching out his arm, he gently pulled her chin up so that she could look at his face. "Arise, o beautiful one from across the sea."

Tiggy tried desperately to hide her gaze from him by averting her eyes. Finding her voice, she replied, "Thank you, kind Pharaoh, for allowing me to come and visit Princess Merira. I have traveled far these many days to reach a friend from long ago."

"Long ago?" he questioned.

"Yes, Your Highness. I came here as a young child and met the princess. It was untimely that I fell ill and was unable to enjoy my visit. However, the princess was gracious enough to ask me to return someday."

48

"Your husband allows you to travel this far unattended?" asked Tuthmosis, narrowing his eyes.

"I have no husband but am attended by my centurions, Your Highness," finished Tiggy, still not looking him in the eye.

Princess Merira caught the gleam in his eye as she announced her unwedded state. She knew that it would be harder for them to find the key if Tuthmosis was constantly requesting their presence.

Tuthmosis said nothing to this but kept his gaze firmly fixed on Tiggy as she continued looking downward, avoiding his eyes. He was intrigued to see her submissively lower her eyes despite her noble stance and proud posture.

"Why do you not look upon the face of the pharaoh?" he finally questioned as he circled her.

"I mean no disrespect, Your Highness. I feel as if you are too mighty to look upon without being granted such favor."

At her words, the pharaoh immediately drew himself up with pride. His ego inflated, he returned to his throne to continue to study this new visitor to the royal household.

Princess Merira, sensing the rising tension within Tiggy, broke in by saying, "My lord, Pharaoh, would you grant us permission to leave? I feel that Princess Amanda is weary from the journey."

With a final long look at Tiggy, he nodded his head and said, "Yes, you must rest. Tonight you will join the royal household for dinner." Waving his hand, he excused them from his presence. Tiggy curtsied as Merira bowed before turning to leave.

Exiting the throne room, Tiggy followed Merira as she led her through the same corridors that she had walked through in her own time. Tiggy began to speak, but Merira quietly warned her not to. "Say nothing, for we have Hessam for a shadow. Come," she said in a louder voice. "Tell me of what you think about the palace."

Tiggy stopped and looked around the beautiful hallway, with its golden wall relief, polished red granite floors, and intricately carved and gilded columns that soared above them to support a towering roof. Running her hand appreciatively over the carving on the nearest column, she turned toward Merira and exclaimed, "It is awe-inspiring, magnificently beautiful … it is all that I imagined and more."

Turning, she saw Merira's outstretched hand. Laughing, Tiggy grasped her hand in her own, saying, "I did not mean to get carried away. It is just that it is incredible for me to behold."

"Yes, it must be," replied Merira, "from what little you have told me already. I am pleased that you love my mother's palace and my father's creation for her."

Lowering her voice a trifle, Tiggy asked, "Senenmut was your father, correct?"

Merira's eyes widened with surprise. "Yes, he was in every sense of the word my father. How did you know?"

"Remember what I spoke of to you before?" Tiggy questioned. Seeing her nod, she continued, "That is how I know."

When they finally reached the end of the corridor, Merira led her outside toward the royal gardens. Tiggy was amazed at the freshness of the air and the difference in the temperature from what she knew to be an Egyptian summer.

Following much the same path that Tiggy, Nikki, and Ian had taken the previous day, they crossed into the gardens. Tiggy gasped as she saw the beautiful trees and flowers blooming in abundance. The statues and fountains were just what one would expect to see on the palace grounds of a powerful pharaoh.

Seeing Tiggy's delighted response, Merira said, "I thought that you would wish to see this. Tell me, for I gather from your expression, does it not look like this in your time?"

"No," said Tiggy as her eyes darted from place to place, "not even remotely the same. It is all sand and crumbling rock. "

"Well, let us enjoy it while you are still here." Clapping her hands, she said to the slaves, "Quickly … bring food and drink for us."

Turing to Tiggy, she said, "It is warm. Come … let us bathe while we wait for them to return."

Tiggy was willing to do anything that Merira wanted to do, especially since she depended on Merira for everything.

Hours later, Tiggy returned to the rooms she had been allotted. Upon entering, she noticed that Ian was pacing the floor and Nikki was lying on some cushions, eating more dates.

Spying her, Ian exclaimed, "Finally! I've been worried that something had happened to you."

Tiggy looked surprised. "If something had happened to me, then it would have happened to you two as well."

"What have you been doing?" asked Nikki, his mouth full of food.

"Well, to start with, I met Tuthmosis III, then toured the palace, went for a swim in the gardens, ate some lunch, and then returned here."

"You met Tuthmosis?" blurted out Ian. "Are you insane?"

"No!" replied Tiggy with a scowl on her face. "He knew we were here, so Merira and I thought it best to meet him and get it over with now."

"This whole thing is insane … crazy," stated Ian, running his hands through his hair in frustration.

"What do you mean?" asked Nikki.

"Think about it: we traveled through time because we connected some pieces of gold together, we're pretending to be people we're not, and we've got to find more pieces to leave this place. I mean, am I the only one concerned here?"

"No," replied both Nikki and Tiggy.

"But we've got to do the best in the situation we're in," continued Tiggy. "We've got to rely on Merira."

Nikki continued to watch the two of them argue back and forth as if he were watching a tennis match. Wisely, he said nothing; he just kept eating.

"I would think that it was obvious that's what we've got to do," she said while removing her veil. "Certainly you are not that obtuse to think that we could do anything in this century on our own and undetected. Maybe I should be asking you if you are insane," she said as she noticed Nikki pointing to her hair.

"What?" she asked Nikki as he continued to motion to her hair while trying to swallow what was in his mouth.

"Your hair," said Ian, grabbing the veil and covering her blonde hair quickly.

"I just wanted to take it off for a moment," said Tiggy defiantly. "It was beginning to bother me."

Nikki found his voice and ventured, "Don't forget what Merira said."

"I know," Tiggy declared as she went to a mirror and readjusted her veil. "It really looked strange swimming in it. This is one of the few things that I hate about being here."

"Not to change the subject," said Ian, now sitting down, "but do you have the faintest idea where to begin looking for this clue?"

"Not the slightest," she replied as she sat down beside Nikki on the cushions. "I don't even know what the clue is, and I am hesitant to take out the other pieces to read the hieroglyphic inscriptions on their backs."

"Why?" questioned Nikki. "It's not as if they didn't make those pieces in the first place."

"Actually, Nikki, Tuthmosis did not make the pieces. Hatshepsut commanded her royal vizier to make them after she had the dream that foretold her that she would need to hide her wealth."

"But, Tiggy," he continued, "why don't we just find this royal vizier and have him tell us what and where the piece or pieces are that we need?"

"For two reasons: one, we don't know if we can trust him; and two, he hid the treasure and is not about to go telling some strange people from another time where to find it."

"Oh, I never thought of that," he returned with a shrug of his shoulders. "By the way, don't you think we need to be speaking in Egyptian or Arabic or something? Don't you think that they'll detect that we're not what they think we are?"

At his question, Tiggy and Ian both laughed aloud. Nikki was somewhat confused by their laughter. "Why's that question so funny?"

"Well, for starters, Nikki, we're supposed to be from another country, Rome to be exact. Second, no one in this century could ever even hope to understand us," answered Ian.

"I don't understand," he said with a quick shake of his head.

"It's like this," Tiggy said. "No one will speak English for the next two thousand years at least, so there's no way that anyone will ever understand what we are saying to each other. That's the reason why I have to translate everything for you to Merira. She has no idea what you are saying. I can understand her only because I have studied the ancient language for years now."

"Oh, I never thought of that," returned Nikki, now smiling. "Say, that's great! No one can understand us. I love it!"

Rising to her feet, Tiggy announced, "I'm going to rest. I have a royal dinner to attend tonight at the pharaoh's request."

"What?" exclaimed Ian and Nikki.

"Yes, I'm afraid so," said Tiggy with a shrug. "I was politely yet forcefully told that I would be joining the pharaoh for dinner."

"By whom?" asked Ian.

"By Tuthmosis, of course," she finished while walking from the room. "Now, let's see if this reed-woven mattress is any good."

Several hours later, Tiggy awoke with a start. *Where am I?* she thought. Then the memories of what had occurred struck her like a tidal wave. She knew that she needed to quickly find the next clue, join the pieces, and get them out of this ancient century and back to their own time before history would be changed forever.

I just need to read the inscriptions on those pieces and see if they contain any clues about where to go from here, she thought as she rose from her bed to search for Nikki and Ian.

She paused in the doorway when she saw them sound asleep on the cushions. She smiled as she thought of how Nikki had desperately wanted an adventure. "Well, you certainly got more than you bargained for," she whispered.

Quietly crossing the room, she opened the small bag that held Ian's things and began searching for his small magnifying glass. Without moving or opening his eyes, Ian said, "Need something?"

Tiggy jumped backward. "Goodness, you startled me, and yes, I need your magnifying glass. I was going to read the inscriptions on the backs of the other pieces before dinner. Hopefully, that'll give us some idea of where to begin."

After finding the glass, she sat next to Ian on the cushions. He sat up and moved over, making room for her. He watched as she drew out a small bag that she had tied with a string and put around her neck. Inside were the four pieces that they had found earlier in their adventure. She opened the bag and poured out the thick, sturdy pieces onto her lap.

She cautiously placed them side by side but did not allow the pieces to join together, for fear they would be transported back through time. Picking up the pieces, she began to study the inscriptions under the magnifying glass.

Ian patiently sat and watched her as she picked up each piece and studied it. "Anything?" he asked.

"Yes, but I am afraid it's not much help," she responded as she returned two of the pieces to the bag and slipped it back inside her dress.

"Aren't you forgetting the other two?" he asked, pointing to the two still resting on her lap.

"No, actually I'm not. I think it would be better if I didn't have all the pieces. I feel that you need one, and Nikki needs to carry one too. That way, if anything does happen, the pieces won't fall into the wrong hands," she concluded.

"Good thinking," Ian said. "Now, what clues do we have to go on?"

"Clues … you found more clues?" asked Nikki, rolling over.

"Yes, but I'm not so sure they are going to help us," said Tiggy with a shrug.

"Why?" asked Ian.

"Well, one piece, the scarab, talks of the ankh, which is practically everywhere in Egyptian culture. The other piece, the auta, speaks of the goddess of Nekhbet, which is represented by a vulture."

"Let me guess," said Nikki. "It's everywhere too."

"No, not everywhere, just usually surrounding the pharaoh," answered Tiggy with a knowing look of dismay.

"Surely the royal vizier wouldn't make a piece that would end up in the pharaoh's possession," interjected Ian.

"Why not?" she retorted. "After all, the best place to hide something is in its most obvious location; it's usually overlooked."

As she handed one of the pieces to Nikki, he looked up in surprise. "Why are you giving me this?"

"Because," said Tiggy, "I don't want to carry all the pieces if something should happen. Just put it in a bag and put it inside your clothing, making sure that you tie it to yourself in some way. It wouldn't do if one of those pieces got lost."

"I understand," nodded Nikki as he took the pharaoh's crook piece.

Suddenly the door opened, and in stepped Merira. "Greetings, everyone. I brought some more food for your magi and some silks and jewels for you, Amanda."

Seeing the lovely cloth, Tiggy rose to her feet and took it from the handmaiden. "It is beautiful. Thank you, Merira. I will wear it tonight."

"I also brought one of my handmaidens to anoint you with perfume and perform any other duties you may require. I will sit while you dress, for the time is near for the summons to the great room."

Tiggy retired to the other room, leaving Ian and Nikki to entertain the princess. Tiggy unrolled the silk and began wrapping and twisting it around her body until she had achieved a beautiful replica of a Roman toga. She rummaged in her bag and found some of her own beautiful gold jewelry and put the pieces on her wrists, on her ears, and around her throat. She next found a beautiful silk sash that could go in her hair. She quickly brushed her hair free from its confines and allowed it to cascade over her shoulders. With the sash, she made a band and placed it around her head just behind her ears. She let the sash trail down her back, almost to her waist. The effect was stunning, and she knew that this effort was necessary to allow her to get close to the pharaoh; she did not inform Ian that the inscription clearly stated that she would have to get the piece from the pharaoh himself. She applied some soft pink lipstick to enhance her own pink lips and a light dusting of powder across her nose. She sprayed on her own perfume and closed her bag. Taking a deep breath, she left the room to rejoin the others.

At her entrance, everyone gasped; Ian found his voice first.

"Tiggy, no! You need to cover your hair now! You're putting everyone in danger."

"Ian, trust me! I know what I've got to do, and this is one way to do it, irrespective of what Merira says."

Merira watched and listened as the two spoke to each other in a strange tongue. She watched in fascination as they talked adamantly with each other. She saw the gleam of satisfaction in Tiggy's eyes and knew that she had won the battle with her magi.

Merira listened to Tiggy's explanation and said finally, "I hope that you are right in doing this, and I must say that you look beautiful dressed as you are. No one at the royal court will have ever seen anything close to what you have on, which is good, because they will never know that the silk came from Egypt. If you are ready, let us go, for that was the gong announcing dinner for the royal household."

Tiggy looked at Ian and Nikki. "Say a prayer—say several, in fact—that this works."

With that, Merira and Tiggy walked through the double doors to the hallway that would lead them to Tuthmosis.

CHAPTER NINE

▼

The tall, heavy wooden doors opened outward by the waiting sentries to admit Tiggy and Princess Merira into the great dining hall. Merira held Tiggy's hand as they entered and gave her a slight squeeze for confidence as the entire assembly—which consisted of the royal household of Tuthmosis, ranking nobility from surrounding palaces, and the musicians and slaves attending the great table—fell silent at their arrival.

Tiggy held her head proudly as she followed Merira along the entire length of the great table, past all the noble guests dressed in their finest silks, linens, and jewels, to sit beside the pharaoh. Merira bowed to Tuthmosis, explaining their tardiness. "My lord, Pharaoh, please excuse our lateness, for when I saw Princess Amanda, I was taken away by the beautiful clothing she wore and asked her to show me how she tied the garment around herself."

The pharaoh rose to his feet, his eyes still wide with surprise and admiration at the sight of Tiggy. "Princess Merira, sit on my left; Princess Amanda of Rome, you must sit on my right."

Tiggy inwardly smiled with delight as she caught the look in the pharaoh's eyes as she curtsied. Tuthmosis still stared at her as she rose. She quickly lowered her gaze and sat down within inches beside him on a golden chair covered with a silken cushion.

The pharaoh continued staring, and no one spoke until Merira asked pleasantly, "Why do not the musicians play something cheerful upon their strings?"

At her words, Tuthmosis clapped his hand, demanding the musicians to play. "Everyone eat and enjoy themselves, for the festival is at hand."

Immediately everyone began talking about the much-anticipated festival that would be taking place at Karnak. It was an annual event that everyone—young or old, rich or poor, slave or free—enjoyed. There was much celebration and gaiety to be seen, heard, and had.

Merira turned to the royal vizier sitting on her left and inquired, "Are you not excited by the upcoming delight of traveling on the royal barge up the Nile?"

Readily he responded, "Yes, of course, most gracious Princess. I must thank you for the honor that you have bestowed upon me to travel with the pharaoh and you."

Both Tiggy and Tuthmosis remained quiet. He continued to study her while she ate her fish prepared with dates and nuts in silence. He was even more fascinated by her now than he had been when he met her that morning. He marveled at the beauty of her hair; the temptation was too great for him to ignore. Reaching out his hand, he touched the wavy strand that caressed her shoulder.

Tiggy, intently focused on her food and the musicians playing a joyous tune upon their flutes and strings, jumped at his touch. She glanced up quickly; her gaze caught his, and he was captivated. Never had Tuthmosis seen eyes that were blue like the waters of the sea. Leaning closer to her, he quietly declared, "You are a rare gem to be treasured above all the gold and wealth of the earth."

"Your Highness, surely you don't expect me to believe such nonsense," she remarked as she returned her attention to her food.

He ran the silken strands of hair through his fingers again. "Never has Amun-Ra blessed a woman more greatly than you. He took the rays of the sun and touched your hair. He took the blue of the sea and placed it in your eyes. You are an enchantress like nothing I have ever seen."

As she looked up, her eyes held such wonder that he was captivated even further. Tuthmosis knew he would not win this maiden the way he wished, or by any means other than by time, for the look within her eyes told him so. Capturing her hand in his, he said, "Come on the royal barge to the festival. It is on the rising of the second sun. You will enjoy it greatly, and you must tell me if you have anything equal to it in Rome."

"Thank you, Your Highness, for the invitation, but I think I must ask Princess Merira if I may join you."

"Nonsense. She will be attending, and if I command it, then you must come," he finished rather pompously.

She paused a moment and then began by questioning Tuthmosis. "Are you *commanding* me to attend this function at Karnak?"

"Yes, I am *commanding* you if you do not wish to come, but I am *inviting* you if you wish to do so," he finished, astounded that anyone would challenge him.

Raising her chin a trifle in defiance, she replied, "I will think upon whether I wish to attend, for I am not in the habit of being commanded by anyone."

He stared at her incredulously at first and then, sensing her spirit, burst out laughing. He observed the gentle dignity in which she clothed herself, as the eyes of the assembled guests glanced in her direction. She sat proudly with her chin held high until the moment had passed.

Merira glanced across the table, saw Tiggy's aloof countenance, and intervened. "Pharaoh, may we not have the dancers attend us now?"

At the pharaoh's nod, the group of male and female dancers emerged with great energy and enthusiasm. For several minutes, Tiggy forgot that Tuthmosis sat mere inches away from her. She watched and listened as the dancers twirled, swayed, clapped, and sang to energetic song. Their brightly colored clothing, in hues of blue and red, barely covered their bodies, but no one seemed to think anything about it. The movements were somewhat familiar with each other and no one seemed to mind. She assumed that the skimpy clothing and intimate dancing were customary. Everyone was enjoying themselves, and the wine seemed to flow even more freely than it had before the performance began.

After the dancers left, accompanied by thunderous applause, some ladies came in with baskets full of slithering cobras; the snakes emerged from their reed-woven baskets, swaying and sliding across the floor to the hypnotic music of a flutelike instrument. The ladies moved closer and closer to where Tuthmosis sat, bringing the swaying snakes with them. As the snakes came closer, Tiggy quickly rose to her feet and asked to be excused.

She gave a sketchy curtsy, and before the pharaoh could give her permission to leave, she ran out of the room toward the terrace.

Everyone in the assembly turned and watched her, amazed that she would leave before the pharaoh had excused her. Her garments flowed enchantingly around her form as she quickly fled down the terrace steps and out of view.

Tuthmosis rose to his feet to follow her, commanding everyone to stay and enjoy the entertainment.

She continued walking through the bright moonlight until she reached the large bathing pool in the garden. She looked down into the water, trying to calm her racing heart. She had predicted that Tuthmosis would follow, but she was surprised to hear his voice behind her so soon.

"Why did you flee from the performance?" he demanded.

"I am sorry, Your Highness, but I have a great fear of snakes." Looking into his eyes, she declared, "I meant no disrespect to you, sire."

The moonlight shone directly on her face, leaving his in shadow. Her inability to discern his features put her at a disadvantage. She was unprepared for his next move, which was to brush her cheek with his hand. "Your fear of snakes has granted you forgiveness."

Catching her fluttering hand in his, he declared, "You tremble greatly from your fear. How long have you been afraid?"

"Most of my life, sire. I was bitten as a child and have never forgotten the experience. I am sorry to have reacted so."

Tuthmosis continued to stare at her as she turned from him; her profile was just as beautiful as the rest of her. "Your hair reflects even the glory of the heavens." Running his hands through it, he stated, "It is as soft as the down of a newborn duckling. You are unique among your kind?"

"Yes, Your Highness, there are some but not many with my coloring," she answered as she began to walk away from him toward a nearby stone bench.

"You run from me? Why?" he asked of her gently.

"I have heard from Merira that she is to be your God Wife," she returned as she seated herself upon the bench. "Would she not think it strange if I became fond of someone to whom she was to marry? She is my friend; I wouldn't do such a thing."

The pharaoh looked puzzled by this and did not respond right away. Then, walking over, he stood before her and said, "A man can have more than one wife."

Tiggy shook her head. "No, I would never be so dishonored as to allow my husband to have another wife."

Tuthmosis was shocked by this. "In Rome, men have only one wife?"

She nodded. "If one truly loves, then you cannot give your heart to more than one, for someone will always be without love for a time."

"Are you without love now?" he asked.

"Yes, Your Highness," she replied quietly.

"I do not believe the men in your Rome have eyes with which to see," declared the pharaoh forcefully.

Tiggy laughed. "You say the oddest things to me, sire."

"You do not believe me?" he asked.

Tiggy immediately realized her mistake and slid off the bench to her knees. Bowing her head, she replied, "I am sorry, Your Highness. I did not mean to disbelieve you. The disbelief is within me."

Reaching down, he pulled her to her feet. "You are a strange one, beautiful Amanda from Rome. I have never met one such as you. Come ... let me show you my palace."

Over the next several hours, Tuthmosis gave Tiggy a tour of the palace; his magi were never far from his side. Tiggy asked him if they needed to return to his guests. "I am Pharaoh. I do as I please. There is good wine and beautiful women. Do not worry. They will find a way to amuse themselves."

"Yes, sire," she replied as he handed her a drink given to him by one of his magi.

"Drink this, and tell me if you think the wine is not from the god Amun-Ra."

She placed the golden goblet to her lips and glanced at the magi that had handed it to Tuthmosis. His eyes seemed to narrow as her lips touched the rim. An evil look crossed his face, and Tiggy sensed a warning in her head. She pretended to drink from the goblet but actually only touched the golden wine to her lips to show moisture.

"This indeed is quite delicious, but there is an odd taste to it," she replied as she looked at the head magi. He gave her a hard look in return as the pharaoh took her hand to continue the tour.

After passing through several more doors and passing several more magi, they entered an enormous and luxurious set of rooms containing golden couches, exotic woods, and fine linen.

"This is the royal suite," announced Tuthmosis as he led her out onto the balcony.

An alarm sounded in her head as she sensed that Tuthmosis had romantic intentions. She gently pulled her hand from his grasp and wandered to the far side of the balcony. "Look … you can see the garden and all of the guests from here. It is breathtakingly beautiful."

"As are you," he declared as he approached. She nervously placed the wineglass against her lips, remembering at the last moment just to moisten them. Pulling the goblet from her hands, he placed it on the railing and pulled her into his arms.

Her eyes grew wide as she whispered faintly, "No, Your Highness. This is not right. It is not fair to Merira; she is to be your wife." Placing her hands against his chest, she pushed herself away while she devised a plan.

She walked to the farthest corner of the balcony and stared at Tuthmosis, who was coming toward her. She grew fearful as his image began to blur, and she grew light-headed. Suddenly she uttered, "I feel very weak. I cannot see clearly."

Tiggy's eyes widened in fear and confusion as she began to sway before him. Her eyes became fixed and vacant. He quickly traversed the distance between them as she reached out to grab the railing and missed. He caught her in his arms as she fell. "The wine …," she murmured as her eyes closed. "It tasted strange."

"Princess Amanda," shouted Tuthmosis as he felt her body grow limp. Picking her up in his arms, he shouted for his magi. "Quickly, go and fetch the princess and bring her here. Say nothing of this to the guests."

He walked swiftly to the nearest couch and laid her down upon it. He picked up her hand, which was cold, almost lifeless, and placed it against his chest to warm it. He began shouting orders to the magi, who remained in the room.

Tiggy was promptly covered, and the wine was brought to the pharaoh. Remembering her words, he sniffed the wine. *It does have a strange aroma*, he thought. He carried the goblet to his ibis and allowed the bird to drink from it. Moments later, the creature fell over, dead. "Poison!" he declared. "Who would dare to poison a guest of the pharaoh, much less the beautiful woman I intend to be mine? Death will come swiftly to the one who tried to destroy what is mine."

"Death?" shouted Merira as she came into the room. Seeing Tiggy's inert form, she ran toward her. "Princess Amanda? What has happened?" she questioned as she knelt down beside her. "Pharaoh, we must get her magi. Maybe this is something that occurs often; she was unwell as a child."

"As you wish," declared the pharaoh as he waved for them to do as the princess bade. "I do not believe that this is an illness, for the wine she had killed the ibis."

"What!" exclaimed Princess Merira. "Who would wish to kill the princess? She only arrived today."

"This I will find out, for death cannot take her yet. It is too soon for one such as her. Send a priest to her room to attend her," he commanded.

A handmaiden brought Princess Merira a bowl of water and a linen cloth, which the princess used to bathe Tiggy's face, for she had started to perspire and shake. Merira wiped her forehead as Tuthmosis paced around her, muttering his intention to kill the one who would harm her. The door burst open to admit two worried-looking people. Immediately Ian ran to Tiggy's side and began trying to revive her; he took the linen cloth from Merira and wiped her face while begging her to awaken. Nikki stood helplessly at the end of the couch as he looked upon her pale and unresponsive face.

Tuthmosis watched in wonder at these two as they spoke in a strange tongue to one another. He also caught the look on Ian's face as he watched Tiggy. "This man, her magi, obviously has feelings for the princess," Tuthmosis said to Merira. "He is unworthy of her."

"Ian, what is wrong? What has happened to Tiggy?" cried out Nikki, ignoring the pharaoh and princess.

"I have no idea. I don't speak their language. I don't understand what the princess is trying to say," he moaned as the princess motioned to him.

"These two do not understand you, great Pharaoh, because they are the ones spoken of in the dream," snarled Hessam, the head magi to the pharaoh.

"Nonsense," interjected the princess vehemently. "I know Princess Amanda, and she comes from far away in Rome. I knew her when she was a small child."

"If this is true, Princess," Hessam said slyly, "then where is her royal escort, her servants, her slaves? Why is she attended by only a boy and a single magi?"

"This I do not know, but I am sure there is an answer to your question—not that you have any right to question a friend of mine." Glancing at Tuthmosis, Merira could see that Hessam's words were taking root. "Oh, great Pharaoh, can we not discuss this if Princess Amanda lives? I fear for her and would like to remove her to her rooms."

"Yes," he said as he waved to her magi to take her from the room. He observed the tenderness on the face of the one who carried her and the anguish on the boy's. His eyes narrowed as his gaze met Hessam's. *Did he poison the wine, or did someone else? Did his words ring with truth, or were they jealous lies?* thought Tuthmosis as he watched the magi depart with Princess Amanda.

Hours later, Tiggy opened her eyes to see an anxious group sitting by her bedside. She tried to sit up, but Ian was immediately by her side, urging her to lie back down.

"How do you feel?" Ian inquired.

"I feel tired. I really want to move around, yet I don't. What happened to me?"

"Tell us what you remember," interjected the princess, unable to wait while Tiggy talked with Ian and Nikki.

"I think the wine was poisoned, and I believe that Hessam may have done it."

The princess sat in silence, pondering her words, as Tiggy retold the same story to Ian and Nikki in English.

"It has to be Hessam," Ian said. "Or at least he ordered it to be put in the wine that you would drink. Do you think he suspects you?"

"I most certainly do!" she retorted. "Throughout dinner, I noticed him watching me, and then when I went out into the garden and Tuthmosis followed, he looked incensed."

"Why were you in the garden at night with the pharaoh?" asked Nikki.

"I fled because the snakes scared me! You know that I'm terrified of snakes, despite the fact that I walked through those horrible things to get the chest. I had fire then to keep them away, but at the banquet I had nothing."

Ian scowled when he heard this but chose to say nothing. He did not like the fact that Tiggy was using herself as bait to obtain one of the clues. He felt that she had not told him everything about the piece that she was determined to go after; he knew that she wouldn't have taken the risk of revealing her hair and features unless she intended to acquire the piece from the person who had it—the pharaoh himself.

Princess Merira interrupted his thoughts as she loudly asked Tiggy if she felt well enough to go bathing. Tiggy stared at her, trying to make sense of the hidden meaning of her words.

"What did she ask?" inquired Nikki.

"She wants me to go bathing with her," Tiggy replied.

"Is she crazy?" Ian asked. "You almost died from being poisoned last night, and now she wants you to get out of bed and go swimming?"

"Before you get too worked up, Ian, I think she has a reason for doing this that she cannot express in these surroundings. I, for one, have noticed the shadows on the terrace outside. There is a constant patrol of magi around this room."

"I think Merira suspects that they are eavesdropping on her," announced Nikki as he walked toward the great open door that led to the terrace. Turning around, he declared, "It will do them no good to listen to us, because they can't understand us," said Nikki with a laugh, "not even the princess."

When their conversation paused again, Merira pressed Tiggy to go to the garden pool and bathe. "Princess Amanda, I feel that the warmth of the sun and the water will bring back your good health. I don't believe that you would want to miss the trip on the royal barge or the jubilee at Karnak." She looked knowingly at Tiggy. Seeing the gleam in her eyes, the princess knew that Tiggy understood how important it was for them to all attend the festival at Karnak.

"Yes," Tiggy quietly agreed as she rose from her bed, pushing the light blanket to the side. "A swim sounds like a great idea."

Ian and Nikki both protested that she should remain in bed and not be foolish. She waved them aside as she rose to her feet, waiting a moment for the room to stop spinning around her.

"Tiggy, this is foolishness," declared Ian as he caught hold of her arm to steady her.

"Maybe so, Ian, but it is essential that I look like I am recovering. I think that Merira suspects one of the pieces will be at Karnak. How can I find the next clue if I don't go to the festival?"

Nikki blurted out, "We may not return?"

"I don't know, Nikki, but we need to find the two remaining pieces, and then we may leave to return home."

"You're right," interjected Ian. "We must get the pieces and leave as quickly as possible. If you are going swimming, we will stay with you to make sure nothing dangerous takes place."

"That is perfectly acceptable to me," declared Tiggy as she walked unsteadily over to the slave holding the clothes that Merira had brought and began unwrapping her toga. "If you guys will excuse me, I need to change." With that announcement, they walked from the room and waited on the terrace for her to change.

Chapter Ten

▼

Ian carefully placed Tiggy at the water's edge, saluted, and then walked away from the two ladies. He wanted to stand guard far enough away to be able to survey the palace gardens and those potentially walking or hiding within it.

The sounds of laughter and splashing, which could be heard for yards in the stillness of the day, drew the attention of Tuthmosis as he walked from the Shrine of Hathor. The sounds were like a siren song, leading him away from the temple of the priest.

Upon his entering the garden, Ian noticed that the pharaoh's eyes feasted on the sight of Princess Merira and Tiggy splashing and acting like young children in the bathing pool.

His magi had informed him that Princess Amanda was alive but had yet to leave her bed. He could now see that they had been mistaken. Her face, upturned with laughter, was a sight to behold, and he noticed that he was not the only one intent on watching the childish display. Across the great pool stood one of her magi, who never took his eyes off her. He wondered about this magi, who seemed to watch his royal princess with eyes full of something more than mere loyalty. It was a curiosity that he chose to study. He also noted that Hessam watched from another side of the garden, and he too never looked away from this princess from Rome.

Tuthmosis decided to intrude upon them. "Good day to you, my royal princesses. I am glad to see that you are feeling better this day," he said, gesturing toward Tiggy.

"Thank you, Your Highness," she replied as she sank down into the water up to her neck, trying to hide herself from his penetrating gaze.

Princess Merira stepped out of the water and made her way toward a chaise lounge of sorts. "Come, Amanda. We will eat, for I see that the slaves have brought us our midday meal," she announced.

Tiggy signaled Ian to attend her. He quickly covered the ground between them and kept his eyes averted from her subserviently as he neared the pool's edge. "Do you need something?" Ian asked.

"May I have a towel please?"

Ian gave a Roman salute, a slow smile spreading across his features. "I should hope so, dear Princess Amanda. It might be too, uh, revealing," he finished with a laugh.

Tiggy swatted the water and covered his retreating back with a great splash. When she swam away to await her towel, she caught the look of confusion on the pharaoh's face. She blushed under his intense gaze. Choosing to avoid it, she dove underwater and swam to the far side of the pool, away from him and his knowing looks.

She had to admit that the water had revived her tired body, and she did indeed feel hungry. However, she did not feel comfortable with the way the pharaoh's eyes devoured her wherever she went. Therefore, she decided to swim above and under the water until Nikki returned. Breaking the surface of the water, she started when she saw Tuthmosis before her on the steps that led into the pool. In his hands, he held the robe that she had asked Ian to tell Nikki to fetch for her. Now she would have no choice but to come out of the water under his watchful eye. Swimming toward him, she gave Ian a disappointed look. "Thanks for nothing," she said as he shrugged his shoulders.

Rising from the water, she could feel Tuthmosis's eyes upon her. She quickly reached out for the long robe and covered herself with it. "Thank you, sire," she said as she stepped away from his hands and walked toward Merira, who was lounging and eating in the sun.

Sitting down on the cushions beside Tiggy, Tuthmosis clasped one of her hands in his. "I am glad that you did not enter the afterlife last night. I was in great fear for you, and I am determined to find the person who did that to you."

"Thank you, sire, for your help," she responded shyly. "I do have one question that perplexes me."

"What is that, Princess?" he responded as he leaned closer to her.

"Why would someone wish to murder me? I know no one here except Princess Merira."

"This thought has been troubling me as well. It seems that someone is jealous of your beauty or maybe that I am interested in you becoming my wife."

Both Tiggy and Merira gasped at his announcement. Merira, turning away from everyone, began to cry, leaving Tiggy to deal with the startling confession.

"But Pharaoh, you are to wed Princess Merira. She is your chosen wife. I cannot be your choice, for has not Amun-Ra decreed that Merira would be your God Wife?" asked Tiggy as she rose to her feet and walked to the water's edge.

Tuthmosis joined her as Ian and Nikki moved closer to her side. He immediately sensed their threatening presence and demanded that Tiggy have them withdraw. "Have your magi step away from you! I will not have them listening to what we say."

Turning, she said, "Can you two pretend to give us some privacy? Just go over where you can still hear me."

Ian and Nikki both saluted and walked several paces away. Turning her attention back to Tuthmosis, she said, "My apologies, sire. My centurions are very protective of me, especially after the poisoning of last night, and they feel that anyone could be a threat."

"Ah yes, your magi, or what was the word you called them?"

"Centurions, Your Highness. In Rome, they are called centurions."

Nodding, he said, "Your centurions should protect you, but I am curious, Princess. Where is your royal entourage? Why are you attended by one centurion and a youth?"

Looking up into his eyes with the utmost frankness, Tiggy gave a beautiful performance by telling another lie straight to his face.

"Sire, you care to hear my story?" she asked with wide, innocent eyes that captured him.

"Yes, Princess, I am desirous to hear what finally brought you here so far from home and with no attendants."

"You see, my father, the emperor, wanted me to marry this horribly ugly old man from a principality that Rome was going to conquer or probably has already. I just could not see myself married to such a man as he, for trust me, sire, he's not a real man at all. He's nothing like you," she declared as she lowered her eyes shyly.

The pharaoh puffed out his chest with pride. Walking over to her, he lifted her chin and asked, "Then how did you come to be here?"

"I was desperate to escape, for my father would brook no arguments once he had made up his mind. I knew that I would have to escape or be forced into a life of misery, a life with no love or respect. I do not wish to be any man's chattel but to be his treasure."

"Indeed, a treasure you would be. The gods have shown me the bravery that is in your heart and that you have an intelligent mind, one that any man would boast of."

"You are most gracious in your words, Pharaoh."

"Again, tell me how you came to be here, across a great sea?"

"I remembered that when I was young, Princess Merira had asked me to return to Egypt. I knew that I couldn't hide in my own country, because I was too well known. Therefore, I decided to escape into a country where I would be known by only one. I brought my slave and centurion with me only because they spied me leaving the palace in the dead of night. They sympathized with me for what my father had decreed, and they were vital to my successful journey here. I felt that if they helped me make it to Deir-el-Bahari, Princess Merira would keep my secret safe," said Tiggy as she sat down on a bench.

"Yes, she has. She is most loyal to you, for even last night when challenged she did not reveal your secret," agreed Tuthmosis as he stood in front of her.

"Do you see, Your Highness, why I can't even consider what you announced to us? Princess Merira wants to become your God Wife, and I couldn't dishonor our friendship in such a way."

"I will consider what you say, Princess Amanda, because I am fair and just. I also know that Amun-Ra has decreed this marriage. However, I still wish to possess you, for you are the most beautiful of creatures that Amun-Ra has made," he said as he caressed her cheek and took her hand in his.

"Please, sire," she said, rising to her feet. "It would please me if you would tell Merira that she is still to be your God Wife. I feel that my presence might anger her, and if it does, then I will have no place to hide from the emperor," she finished as she let a tear slide down her cheek.

Tuthmosis was moved by her silent tears and her tenderness for Princess Merira. "I will do so because it pleases you."

"Thank you, sire," responded Tiggy as she drew nearer and placed a gentle kiss upon his cheek. Without looking up, she quickly turned and fled the garden, leaving a startled Ian and Nikki to follow.

Tuthmosis was stunned into immobility by her simple delicate kiss on his cheek. He watched her retreating form as her centurion caught up with her and lent his arm for support.

As Tiggy walked away with Ian and Nikki, she knew that Tuthmosis was intrigued by her innocent kiss and her shyly lowered eyes.

Similar thoughts raced through Ian's mind as he walked with Tiggy on his arm. He could tell that the pharaoh had probably never encountered a woman whom he could not understand or control. He could tell by the confused look on the pharaoh's face that Tiggy was somewhat of an enigma to him.

Tuthmosis touched his cheek again as he thought of how her lips had touched his skin like the gentle brushing of a bird's wing. It was obvious that

Princess Amanda cared for the feelings of Merira but also that she was fearful of having to return to her father. Drawing himself upward, Tuthmosis vowed that she would never marry some ugly old man unworthy of such a treasure as she. Then, remembering his vow, he turned toward Merira to assure her that she was still to be his God Wife in the near future. However, he needed to find a place for Princess Amanda in his life, because he had been unable to find peace since he met her. His greatest desire was to possess her. Walking toward Merira, he knew he would devise a plan that would bring Princess Amanda to his side.

Chapter Eleven

▼

The day was warm and clear, and the air smelled sweet as the breeze drifted across the royal barge. It was a sight to behold: the royal barge filled with the beautiful Egyptian ladies clad in luxurious linen; the men in their short white tunic-like skirts, their feet tucked inside golden sandals; the sun glistening off the shiny wooden deck. The sails were unfurled, and the royal flags bearing the cartouche of Tuthmosis III flew high in the breeze. The royal barge, which was more like a large, long, low sailing ship, was filled with people from the royal household, all seated upon luxurious cushions for the short, beautiful journey up the Nile River. The spirits of everyone aboard were soaring high like the eagles above them. Myriad foods, wines, and dancers kept them entertained. Princess Amanda was given a place of honor beside Pharaoh Tuthmosis III and Princess Merira. Even they seemed to be in a jubilant mood as the pharaoh and the princess waved to their subjects, who shouted praises to them from the shores that were lined with lush, tall reeds and scattered palm trees.

Nikki watched the scene in fascination. People came as close to the shoreline as possible to cheer the sight of their pharaoh, some even climbing the noble palm trees that sprung up occasionally from the water's edge. Cheering, waving, laughter, and shouts of joy from the common people filled the air. Never could he have imagined such sights in all of his days. The procession included as much pomp and pageantry as there was in his own time. It was magnificent to see the wealthy and poor of ancient Egypt come out in force. He knew, however, that when they reached Karnak, they would commence searching for one of the missing pieces, the ankh. But for now, he would enjoy the day before him.

Smiling, he looked up at Ian and caught his ready smile, seeing that he too was enjoying the festivities. Glancing over at Tiggy, he laughed as he noticed her eyes darting from place to place; she was trying to absorb as much as possible so that she would remember this ancient time when they returned to their own.

If they returned to their own time—that was the main uncertainty in this whole adventure that was worrying everyone. He wondered if they would indeed find the missing pieces and return. Would he ever see his parents again, and did they know where he had gone? He felt confident that Tiggy would in fact find the missing pieces. It was the one thing that gave him comfort. He could see by her shining eyes that in spite of their unique and incredible circumstances, she was enjoying seeing the history of this great land unfold before her. *Yes*, Nikki thought, *we will find the pieces and return to our own time! I know it!*

As he turned back toward Ian, his eyes were momentarily blinded by a bright reflection coming from his side.

Not noticing Nikki's gaze, Ian turned slightly, and Nikki noticed the gleam of a brightly polished sword at his side. Nikki's eyes widened with surprise. Rising to his feet, he quickly walked toward Ian.

"Ian, where did you get the sword?" he questioned with astonishment.

"I made it," he declared proudly.

"You're kidding me."

"Not at all," he replied, smiling at the incredulous look on Nikki's face.

"How?" he asked.

"While you were napping yesterday, I went in search of a metal craftsman. When I found him outside the palace, I asked him if I could use some metal and his tools to create a replica of a Roman sword—well, as close as I could come, considering I didn't have the appropriate metal."

"You did an incredible job! I can't believe it … but why the sword?"

"Well, since they tried to poison Tiggy, I felt uneasy about not being able to protect her if we found ourselves in a dangerous situation. We know that someone is out to get us or at least Tiggy, so I felt we needed some kind of weapon."

Nikki said, "I think it's a great idea! I wish you would've made me one."

Just then, Merira motioned Tiggy to join them, and Ian watched as she crossed the royal barge. He also watched the eyes of Hessam as he followed her as well. Ian knew that he was a bad character who would harm her again if given the chance and maybe sooner than they thought.

The journey to Karnak did not take long, but with a full barge and the exuberant people on the shore, the trek to the entrance of the great temple took longer than expected. At first, all Tiggy, Ian, and Nikki could do was stare wide-eyed at its magnificence: the colossal walls covered from top to bottom with chiseled scenes of pharaohs hunting and giving offerings, the tall granite obelisk rising high above the center of the temple to soar into the heavens, the lush green grass and giant date trees surrounding the entire temple.

This is how it should still look, thought Nikki as he tried to take in the beauty and wonder of it all.

From the quay, the ground rose so gradually that they hardly noticed the incline. They walked past the statues that flanked the entrance to the temple of Amun. Each statue had the body of a lion and the head of a ram; these statues often appeared in paintings of Karnak. However, the paintings that they had seen looked nothing like the statues before them. Lush vegetation grew in such abundance that Nikki wondered why the Egyptian government of his day did not do something to bring the land back to its former splendor.

Seeing the trio's evident delight, Princess Merira motioned to Tiggy to join her and the pharaoh. "Come … you and your magi must sit beside me during the ceremony. You will witness what you have never seen before."

"What festival is this, Merira?" questioned Tiggy.

"It is the festival of Opet. You know of it?" she responded.

"Yes, I have knowledge of it, but probably not near what I am going to learn today," she said with a smile as she glanced at the open-air courtyard, which was filled with colossal columns covered with inscriptions.

Tiggy turned to Ian and Nikki while they walked and described to them the festival that they were about to witness.

"This is the festival of Opet, which is held during the second civil month according to the lunar calendar. The fields are temporarily flooded; that explains why all of the people are here. It is believed that Amun will bequeath to his living son, the pharaoh, all his might and power. There'll be a dramatic procession of the people honoring Amun that begins at Karnak and ends at Luxor Temple."

"So, this whole ceremony is to solidify that the pharaoh is king?" questioned Ian.

"Yes, it allows the people to 'forgive' the pharaoh for any wrong he has done throughout the year."

"Tiggy, what are these things that we're passing through so quickly?" asked Nikki.

"These are called pylons, and if my memory serves me well, we should pass through six pylons before we get to a small temple surrounded by an ornamental lake."

"Who's that?" questioned Nikki, pointing to the rather large statue situated on their left.

"I would hasten to guess that it is Tuthmosis I, and around to the left of this should be the sanctuary of Hatshepsut."

Turning around, Ian noticed that as they passed through each set of pylons, the number of people grew smaller and smaller, until there were very few people left that would proceed into the sixth pylon sanctuary.

"Question," said Ian. "Why are there fewer and fewer people?"

"I would guess that it is because we are entering the most sacred of sanctuaries. Look at those obelisks," cried Tiggy. "They are huge."

"And very beautiful," declared Ian.

"They are made completely of red granite, and the one to the left, the tallest, should be Hatshepsut's; it is one solid piece. The sixth pylons, if you notice, have two papyrus and two lotus columns; this symbolizes the unification of Upper and Lower Egypt."

"How do you remember all of this stuff?" asked Nikki in disbelief. "I swear you are a walking history book."

She just smiled and retorted, "Thank you. I take that as a compliment."

"Where are we going now?" whispered Ian.

"Why are you whispering?" asked Nikki. "It's not like they even understand our language."

"Because," declared Ian, "I don't want to draw too much attention to ourselves."

"Remember to be on the lookout for the ankh," Tiggy said. "I have a hunch we're going to find it today."

Both Ian and Nikki nodded as the entourage stopped in the middle of the sanctuary. Princess Merira signaled for them to remain seated while the priest and the pharaoh left the sanctuary and walked past the ornamental lake and into a small chapel.

"What now?" whispered Ian.

"The pharaoh and the priests are going to bathe the image of Amun, dress him in colorful linen, and adorn him with incredible jewelry from the temple treasury. The statue should have magnificent necklaces, bracelets, scepters, amulets, and other gold and silver trinkets. When that is finished, they should place the statue inside a shrine and place that on a barque or boat. They will then bring it back into the sanctuary and from there proceed to carry it throughout the pillared halls and courtyards of Karnak and then out toward Luxor Temple."

Ian smiled and said, "You really are a walking, talking history lesson."

Tiggy just smiled as she watched several priests prepare what appeared to be sacrificial sugar and something that looked like honey on the altar before them.

Princess Merira leaned over and asked, "Are you enjoying yourselves?"

"Yes, greatly," said Tiggy, smiling. "Up to this point, all I could ever do was read about this in a book. Now, history has come to life right before my very eyes. This is quite exciting."

Merira smiled at her enthusiasm. "Come. We will eat dates, fish, and olives while we wait for the pharaoh."

Servants then brought food for the princess. However, Tiggy waved away the slaves bearing great quantities of food.

While Tiggy was busy talking with Merira, Nikki closely watched a priest, who was dressed more ornately than the others, as he picked up a golden piece from the altar upon which the other priests were preparing the food.

He strained his eyes to see. *Was that the ankh?* he wondered. *It looks like it from here.* He decided that he needed to get Tiggy's attention before the priests removed the ankh from the altar.

"Tiggy!" he finally blurted out in perhaps the loudest whisper ever heard.

"What?" she said, turning as Nikki tugged on her arm.

"Look at what that priest has on the altar next to the food they're preparing," cried Nikki.

"I don't see it! What is it?" cried both Ian and Tiggy.

"I think it is the ankh piece that we are looking for," said Nikki.

"You've got to be kidding," said Ian, craning his neck to see.

"No, I think Nikki's right, but how are we supposed to get it with all these people watching?" asked Tiggy.

"I'll just have to borrow it," declared Nikki.

"In front of all these people, magi, and priests?" retorted Tiggy. "I don't think so, Nikki." At his crestfallen expression, she added, "Besides, we need to get the other piece before we can leave, and that one is going to take a little more doing on my part. So," she sighed, "let's think of another way to get it before we leave."

Nikki nodded as he continued to watch the piece.

Ian glanced around, feeling as if they were being watched; sure enough, he again caught Hessam staring at Tiggy and Nikki. Ian sensed that Hessam was up to no good, and he leaned down to tell Tiggy that he would be watching from afar. Because she was busy watching the priests as they lit incense and bowed and chanted in a ritual, she barely nodded at what he said.

Ian stood in the shadow of the great pillar at the back of the sanctuary and continued to watch as Hessam made his way over to where the fish was being prepared for each guest. He watched for several minutes before he saw what he had been waiting for: Hessam poured something over the food from a small vessel.

Waving away the slave, Hessam took the tray and gave it to one of his magi. Ian's eyes never left the platter, which held what he suspected was poisoned food. From there, the magi carried the platter to Tiggy. Ian made his way toward her as she continued to wave it away. He could see that the magi was persistent, and eventually she took the food just to get the man away from her. Ian then rapidly pushed his way through the people either sitting or standing in his way until he took the food out of her hand and threw it away from her.

"Ian, what on earth?" she exclaimed but was instantly silenced as she beheld the look of undisguised fury on his face. She rose to her feet and grabbed his arm as he drew his sword from its sheath.

"Ian, no!" she cried, tugging on his arm.

But he would have none of that. In less than a dozen strides, he was facing Hessam with his naked sword. Pointing it at Hessam, he screamed out, "You're a murderer! You're the one trying to kill Princess Amanda!"

Tiggy was too stunned to move as Hessam drew his own sword and the two men began fighting right in the middle of the crowd. Women screamed, and the men and priests fled with them to the sides of the room as chaos erupted.

Princess Merira rose to her feet beside Tiggy, demanding to know what was wrong with her centurion. "Princess Amanda, I demand an explanation for what is occurring."

"My centurion says that the head magi is the one that tried to murder me and that he was trying to kill me just now."

Some women continued to scream as they, along with everyone else, watched intently the battle between the two swordsmen.

Nikki decided to take advantage of the heaven-sent opportunity and grabbed the ankh piece from the altar table. He stealthily crept toward it, yet he seemed not to be moving at all. As the two men continued fighting nearer to Nikki, he moved toward the table, pretending to be fleeing from them. However, he was not fleeing but being very sly.

He put his back against the stone altar as they fought in front of him. The men drew closer, and he slid around the back of the altar, grabbing the piece in his hand as he went. Crouching behind it, he quickly pulled out the pouch that held the other piece. After stuffing the ankh piece in and drawing the string, he rapidly placed the pouch back inside his clothes.

Quickly he stood up and moved far away from the table to stand beside Tiggy, who was watching the sword fight taking place in front of her. They all watched in disbelief as Ian's sword again and again struck the magi Hessam's sword. Each man's face bore a look of determination. Yet Nikki could see from his vantage point that Hessam's eyes contained a deeper hatred. Ian,

Nikki could tell, was outraged but maintained his cool through precise and accurate hits. It was almost as if he was playing with Hessam, and again and again he pricked Hessam's skin with the tip of his sword—almost, Nikki thought, showing his contempt for the magi while doing so.

Finally, when Nikki thought that Tiggy could not stand any more, Ian sliced through the top of Hessam's arm.

Hessam, it appeared to Nikki, was incensed that he had been wounded first. He lost control and hammered his sword into Ian's with such fury that Nikki felt for sure that Ian would collapse under the sheer force of it. The two men had been at it for at least ten minutes when Nikki saw that Tiggy was going to intervene to stop this fight before someone really got hurt.

As she approached the two men, the other magi rushed and grabbed her by the arms to prevent her interference. She struggled against them, shouting, "Let me go! Unhand me, or the pharaoh will hear of this!"

Still they held on to her tightly as she fought. Nikki, seeing that Tiggy was determined to free herself, jumped into the fray.

"Get your hands off of her!" he demanded as he pounded his fists against one of the magi that held her. The man had an iron grip on Tiggy's arm, and finally Nikki decided just to bite him. As Nikki sank his teeth deep into the man's forearm, the man cried out and instantly released her to grab his injured arm.

Tiggy punched the remaining magi hard in the face, and he let her go. Nikki then saw Tiggy sprinting toward Ian and Hessam, who were still fighting, much to the priests' dismay that this was happening in the temple. She came close enough to Hessam to grab on to his arm and begin to pull him away. "Stop this!" she cried. "Stop this now!"

Hessam stepped back from Ian quickly to push her away from him with such force that she flew against the altar steps, hitting her head against them.

At that very moment, Tuthmosis III entered the sanctuary. His eyes widened as he observed the chaos in front of him: he saw Hessam pushing Tiggy, Tiggy landing on the steps with a thud, the centurion and his magi fighting, her slave hitting his other magi, the men and women huddling against the walls, and Princess Merira standing white with shock amid it all.

"Enough!" he bellowed. "What is all of this?"

At his words, everything became quiet, and the two men immediately stopped fighting. Seconds ticked by as no one spoke. Looking around, the pharaoh cried, "Leave us! Go into the second sanctuary and wait for the festival to continue."

The crowd soon dissipated into nothingness, leaving only Princess Merira, Nikki, Ian, Hessam, a few magi, and Tiggy, who was in a daze on the altar steps. At first, no one moved; they just stood looking at one another, too frightened at what the pharaoh might do.

Not caring, Ian spotted Tiggy on the steps leading up to the altar. Throwing a look toward the pharaoh, he stepped over to where she sat still on the steps.

His movement seemed to bring everyone back to life. Princess Merira went to Tiggy's side, as did Tuthmosis. Tenderly, Ian gathered her up in his arms. Turning her face toward him, he saw a large red welt on her forehead. A priest handed Ian a towel soaked with wine to place on her head. The stinging caused her to blink as she looked at the sea of faces surrounding her.

"Are you all right?" questioned Ian.

"Yes," Tiggy softly replied.

"Why did you interfere?" he asked quietly. "Didn't you know that I was an incredible swordsman at Oxford?"

"No, I didn't," she responded. "I was just afraid that you might get hurt."

Smiling tenderly at her, he said, "I understand."

Now that she was sitting up, the pharaoh and Princess Merira began to address her.

"Princess Amanda, are you feeling up to telling us what this was all about?" said Princess Merira gently as she laid her hand softly against Tiggy's now bruising forehead.

Tiggy looked up hesitantly into Tuthmosis's eyes. She could see his repressed anger, which she thought had been caused by their disruption of the Festival of Opet. But actually he was furious that one of his magi would touch her, much less handle her so roughly.

At her bowed head, he demanded that everyone leave the room except for the centurion. He waited and watched as they made their way across the sanctuary and out into the courtyard. Turning to Tiggy, he asked, "What caused all of this to happen? Do you know?"

"No, Your Highness, I do not," came her whispered reply. "But I will ask my centurion, for it was he who drew his sword on your magi," she answered truthfully.

At her words, Tuthmosis glared at Ian, and before the pharaoh could speak another word, she asked Ian what had transpired that would cause him to attack the head magi.

"I drew my sword on him because I saw him pour liquid from a small vessel onto the food that was to be served to you. He didn't allow the slave to bring it but had one of his magi bring it instead," he responded as he saw her face pale at his words. "I feared that he would succeed in poisoning you, because you took the food off the tray."

"That's why you knocked it from my hand?"

Ian nodded. "I did it only to save you. However, this man must be stopped."

Tuthmosis watched the expression on their faces and began to form his opinion before he even heard what Princess Amanda would say. Her frightened countenance and the centurion's apologetic yet forceful look spoke volumes to him. He patiently waited while the two discussed what had happened.

Finally, Tiggy turned to him and said, "If I may, Your Highness, tell you what occurred."

He nodded as she took a deep breath and relayed the story to him.

While she was discussing the incident with the pharaoh, Ian went to retrieve the poisoned food.

Tuthmosis stared as she unfolded her story, even what occurred before the fight began and her role in what had transpired. With shrewd eyes, Tuthmosis measured up Ian, who stood tall and proud under the scrutiny of his gaze.

When she finished disclosing her story, Ian offered Tuthmosis the tray of poisoned food. Without saying a word, the pharaoh took a piece in hand and walked out toward the ornamental lake. He tossed the food to the geese that swam therein and watched as they greedily gobbled it up.

Ian and Tiggy had followed Tuthmosis to the lake to see what would happen. A glint of triumph shone in Ian's eyes as the geese that had eaten the bread began to act strangely. Tiggy watched in horror as the birds began to squawk and twist in great agony. She turned her back and began to cry as she heard the calls of the other geese to those who were dying. She fled back into the sanctuary and sat upon the steps.

Tuthmosis and Ian watched until the last goose died and then looked into each other's eyes with a newfound understanding that transcended language. The pharaoh nodded and motioned for a priest to take Ian to join the rest while he searched for Tiggy.

He found her sitting on the steps of the altar with her back to him, silently weeping. Sensing her emotions, Tuthmosis knelt down at her side. Taking her hand in his, he quietly said, "I will deal with this. And have no fear; your centurion was wise to protect you from harm."

He watched as her tears splashed down upon his hands; lightly he touched her cheek to brush them away.

At his soothing touch, she looked into his eyes, and her reserve broke down. She threw herself against his chest and burst into tears. Astonished, he could only hold her and allow her to cry. Never had a woman touched him without permission, for it was not done to the pharaoh. He found her childlike trust in him quite to his liking.

Several minutes passed before she could stop crying. She drew back, embarrassed by what she had done. Looking up into his face, she softly asked, "Why does he want to kill me? I have been here only a few days and have never done anything to provoke such hatred."

Tuthmosis stared at her, mesmerized by her beauty. The tears still glistened on her lashes, and her eyes were even bluer against the redness caused by her weeping.

"Of this I do not know, but the punishment will be severe," promised the pharaoh.

Tiggy looked up and suddenly thought of the festival, that the people were outside waiting for it to begin. "I am so sorry … the festival," she simply stated as the tears welled up in her eyes once again.

Tuthmosis said, "It is not ruined, just delayed. I will tell the priests to bring the barque out, and we will begin the procession toward the Temple Luxor," he stated as he wiped away a stray tear that had made its way down her cheek. He stood there, staring down into her eyes, until they heard the sounds of the priest bearing the barque. Touching the injury to her head ever so softly, he asked, "Do you find yourself able to attend the rest of the festival?"

Wiping the cloth gingerly across the gash, she replied, "I would not miss it for anything in this world."

"Good. Then let us go," he replied as he turned and gave her his arm. Following behind were the priest and the barque being carried through the sacred hallways and courtyards of Karnak.

CHAPTER TWELVE

▼

The farther they walked along the wide granite-floored hallways of Karnak, the louder and larger the crowd became around them. Discreetly, Tiggy informed Tuthmosis that Princess Merira should walk behind him instead of her, a foreigner. Stopping and taking a step backward, Tiggy allowed Merira to walk behind Tuthmosis. She waited a few more seconds for them to walk on ahead toward their subjects waiting on the outside of the temple.

Ian and Nikki joined her as they passed through to the last of the inner courtyards toward the entrance of Karnak. Nikki rushed up to greet her with a huge grin on his face.

"What happened? Are you okay?" he questioned.

"Yes, I am fine," she replied. "I'm just going to forget about what happened and enjoy the rest of the day."

"Well, just to let you know," interrupted Ian, "I saw some of the pharaoh's other magi taking Hessam out the back of the temple, bound at the wrists. I suppose that Tuthmosis is going to take care of him."

"Let us hope so," responded Tiggy forcefully.

"Since we're sharing good news," suddenly beamed forth Nikki, "I've just got to tell you that I retrieved the ankh off the priests' table."

Ian and Tiggy's eyes widened with surprise.

"You're kidding me?" said Tiggy.

"No way," smiled Nikki. "I've got the piece right here in my bag," he said while touching his chest.

"But how?" questioned Ian.

"I borrowed it off the table while you were fighting. Everyone was so intent on watching you that they forgot all about the piece on the altar. So, I just slid around the edge and took the piece off without anyone even seeing me."

"That's fantastic!" crowed Tiggy. "We'll take a look at it when we get back to the palace when no one else is around."

Walking through the final entrance of Karnak, they could hear the crowd cheering for the pharaoh. The glaring sun did not seem to deter their enthusiasm as the pharaoh himself began to pull, with leather straps like reins around his shoulders, the barque—which was a highly decorated and gilded wooden box, carrying within it the solid gold statue of the image of the god Amun-Ra draped with the jewels of Egypt—on a skiff across the sand toward Luxor.

The pharaoh, Princess Merira, Tiggy, Ian, and Nikki moved into the crowded streets, where the people elbowed each other to glimpse the sacred vessel. Many small Egyptian children were lucky to be placed on their parents' shoulders in order to be able to see.

They completed the journey on foot, stopping at various resting stations. The people heard the steady beat of a soldier's drums and watched as the Nubians danced to songs of devotion sung by the priests that followed behind the pharaoh.

The journey to the Temple Luxor did not take long, and Ian, Nikki, and Tiggy were entranced with the crowd's response to the entire festival. Upon arriving at Luxor, the pharaoh and the priests left the crowd behind and maneuvered the barque into the darkness of the temple. Incense filled the air as the pharaoh communed with Amun and asked for a plentiful harvest. Tuthmosis emerged from the sanctuary several hours later, and the citizens of Egypt greeted him wildly. Throughout the afternoon, the people praised his accomplishments and forgave all of his wrongdoings. The crowd began to chant, "He was once more the embodiment of divine strength and generosity, the source of bounty and well-being for Egypt."

Princess Merira came and escorted Tiggy, Ian, and Nikki to one side of the temple that allowed them to watch the common people as they came to ask the god questions that could be answered by a simple yes or no. They also watched with interest as the priest distributed loaves of bread and jars of beer to the citizens.

Tiggy also watched in fascination as the priests carried out cakes in the shape of pyramidal obelisks. They looked similar to tiered wedding cakes, and now that Hessam was bound, Tiggy felt like trying a piece to see how it would taste.

Nikki volunteered to get a piece for everyone, while Ian and Tiggy sat and watched the events transpiring around them.

Tiggy turned to Ian and said, "I wish I had some paper to take notes of all that we are seeing and hearing. I have a feeling that I won't be able to remember all of this once we leave—that is, if we can leave."

Ian smiled and retorted, "I feel the same." Looking around he continued, "It's all so overwhelming. I just want to absorb all of it so that I'll never forget it."

Tiggy sighed and nodded her head in agreement. She quickly laughed as she spied Nikki coming with several large pieces of cake in his hands.

Handing a piece to everyone, Nikki sat down on the sand. After taking a large bite, Nikki exclaimed, "This is really good and kind of sugary sweet. I was expecting it to be disgusting, because it looked so dry with no icing on the top, but I was wrong. It tastes a little different, but it certainly is good."

Both Tiggy and Ian agreed as they tasted their cake. Before they were halfway finished eating theirs, Nikki jumped to his feet, declaring, "Man, that was good. I'm going for seconds and maybe even thirds."

Tiggy just smiled and shook her head as Ian asked Nikki to bring him another piece as well.

All day and into the night, they watched as the common people came to have their questions answered and their futures brightened with words of forthcoming good fortune.

Food and wine were brought to them as they strolled through the grounds of the Temple Luxor. Every now and again, they would catch sight of Merira or Tuthmosis III. As night began to fall, the princess finally made her way toward them. Despite being tired from the long day, each greeted her warmly, and each held hopes of returning to the palace for some much-needed sleep.

Merira came toward Tiggy and informed her that they would not be returning to the palace. At her look of dismay, Merira just laughed and explained, "You see, on this night, the pharaoh commands a favored few to join him on the royal barge to sleep. Through the night and morning, we will sail up the Nile to be seen by the people who did not make the journey to Karnak or Luxor."

When Tiggy did not respond, she continued, "Very few are granted such favor, and this should be looked upon as a great *opportunity* for you."

Immediately, Tiggy grasped her meaning and nodded her head in understanding and approval. Tiggy was surprised to hear of this practice, for, in all her research, she had never once read of it. She was fascinated yet again to discover something else that had not been recorded in the annals of history. Turning to Ian and Nikki, she said, "Tuthmosis has invited us to spend the night on the royal barge while it sails up the Nile."

Nikki was excited by the prospect of another new adventure and began to follow Princess Merira toward the spot where chariots waited to take them to the royal barge from Luxor.

Ian, however, was less exuberant.

"I'm not surprised that Tuthmosis wants you to join him on the royal barge," he said, somewhat angrily. At her downward glance, he pressed his point further. "I know that there's something that you're not telling me, something that you are holding back."

She looked at him full in the face and then lowered her eyes again to the sand, unwilling to meet his piercing gaze. Finally, she whispered, "I wish that you would just trust me to do the right thing."

"I do trust you, but placing yourself in danger for the sake of a treasure is not worth it."

"It's not about the treasure anymore, Ian," she said, turning away from him to look at the moon shining high above them.

"Then what is it about?" he persisted.

"It is about our lives."

"Our lives?" he parroted. "What are you saying? Tiggy, I need an answer. I know the hieroglyphics told you something that you're not telling us."

"Yes," she agreed quietly. Then, straightening up, she declared, "It's something that must be done for all of us."

Ian finally admitted defeat, for he knew her well enough to know that when she got that determined look on her face, there was no stopping her.

In silence, they walked across the sand to join the others. Nikki had already boarded a chariot and was waiting for them to join him. As Ian helped Tiggy step into the chariot, a magi came over to speak to her.

"Princess, pharaoh sent me to get you," the magi said. "You are to ride to the royal barge with him."

She nodded and stepped down, saying, "Here we go. Better to begin now before I lose my nerve." Without another word, she followed the magi.

"What's she talking about?" questioned Nikki.

"I think I know, but I don't want to say," retorted Ian as he grabbed the reins and started to follow the other chariots without a backward glance toward Tiggy.

Sensing Ian's anger, Nikki wisely remained quiet for once.

Meanwhile, Tiggy followed the magi across the sand to where the pharaoh was waiting. His eyes brightened as she arrived, and a sudden smile lessened the harshness of his angular features. She smiled in return.

"You have enjoyed this day," said the pharaoh.

"Yes, aside from the scene earlier today, it was wonderful," she answered truthfully. Her eyes widened when she beheld the Nekhbet, which he now wore around his neck. "It was only a little lonely," she added as she lowered her eyes to his chest to avoid looking into his eyes, fearful that he might notice her interest in the piece.

"There is no need for you ever to be lonely, my beautiful one."

She peeked up at him through her lashes and was astonished to see the intensity of emotions written clearly on his face.

Stepping closer, he took her hand into his, astonished that it was in fact quite cold. He felt her shudder as he ran his hands down her bare arms. "Come … you are cold," he said as he guided her into his chariot.

She moved to the front of the chariot and was not surprised when the pharaoh stepped close behind her. As he wrapped his arms around her waist, she looked up at him over her shoulder. She drew in her breath as she saw the look in his eyes. Losing her nerve, she turned around.

At her response, the pharaoh only stepped closer and wrapped his arms tighter around her. They rode this way all the way back to the royal barge. When they arrived, Ian looked at how close the pharaoh was to Tiggy, and his lips compressed into a thin line. Dismounting from the chariot, Ian lost no time in crossing over to the pharaoh's chariot, intent on freeing Tiggy from the pharaoh's embrace.

Tuthmosis stepped down and turned to help Tiggy alight from the chariot. As her foot touched the sand, she looked up to catch the expression on Ian's face. She sucked in her breath and prayed that he would not do anything foolish. Holding out his hand, she reached for it. However, Tuthmosis had other ideas and placed her hand upon his and escorted her toward the barge. Ian could only follow.

Without turning, Tuthmosis commanded, "Have your centurion withdraw with your slave. His presence is not required, for I wish to be alone with you."

She nodded and said, "As you wish." Turning to Ian, she said, "Take Nikki and find out where we are to sleep tonight. Tuthmosis wants you to go away." Seeing that his immediate response was going to be one of protest, she hurriedly said, "Please, Ian, don't fight this and do something foolish. Like it or not, I've got to get the last piece from the pharaoh himself."

Ian curtly bowed toward her without saying another word. She could tell that he was immensely angry yet was wise enough to let things be.

Despite the turmoil going on within her, Tiggy was delighted to see the transformation of the royal barge. Small luxurious tents had been erected on the deck of the barge. Pausing to look around, Tuthmosis inquired, "You are pleased?"

"How could I not be? It's like nothing I have ever beheld," she said in a pleased voice in spite of herself.

"Very few are on board, and we should not be disturbed," he stated as she walked toward where Nikki was standing.

Pretending not to understand, she said, "Disturbed, Your Highness? I should think not, for after such a long day, everyone would be seeking his or her sleep."

Taking her hand in his, he drew her toward a raised section at the back of the barge. Nikki started to follow, but she shook her head for him to stay behind. Upon mounting the steps, Tuthmosis guided her to the farthest point that jutted out over the water. Releasing her hand, he stepped very close to Tiggy and said, "You know that I long to possess you."

"Sire, you must not say these things to me," she protested, turning away from him to look out upon the water. "You know that the princess is to be your God Wife in less than one lunar month. Please do not put me in the position of having to hurt her."

Tuthmosis stared down into her worried eyes. "Why do you continue to resist me? Merira does not care if I have you. All she wants is to be the wife of the pharaoh. She cares nothing for me."

She declared, "That is not true. She does care about you, and I have told you already that I do not wish to be any man's possession."

"Possession?" he cried in disbelief. "You would never be that to me."

"Maybe not, sire, but I still would not hold a position of respect in your household. Being of royal blood myself, I would not settle for anything less."

Seeing that she was in earnest, he banged his fists upon the railing. "Why do you persist to defy and confound me?" he shouted as he grabbed hold of her upper arms brutally. She feared that his grip would leave bruises on her arms.

"Please, Your Highness, you must try and understand! You are asking of me that which I cannot give," she begged as tears stung her eyes from the intense pressure he was placing on her arms.

Glancing down into a pair of sorrowful eyes only seemed to infuriate him further. Determined to take what he wanted, he roughly pulled her to himself and kissed her. He felt the wetness of her tears on his face, and he abruptly released her.

Her strength gone, she sank to the deck while tears coursed down her cheeks. Looking down at her pathetic form, he turned and walked away in frustration.

Tiggy sat upon the deck for a long time, mulling over what had occurred. A great sadness overwhelmed her. Not only had she made a mess of things with Tuthmosis, but also Ian was furious with her. *What am I to do now?* she contemplated as she rose to her feet and walked to the railing. *How can I fix this mess that I have gotten myself into this time?*

Seeing no immediate answers to her questions, she turned toward her tent to get some much-needed sleep. Her attention was arrested by a slight bumping noise below the deck. Leaning over slightly, she noticed a boat tied to the back of the barge. "Curious," she muttered. Shrugging her shoulders, she turned to go.

Turning around, she came face-to-face with several men draped all in black. Before she could even draw in her breath to scream, the man nearest her quickly clamped his hand over her mouth and drew a sharp knife, placing it against the base of her neck. Her eyes grew wide with fright as she saw the moonlight glimmer on the blade. She could feel her wrists being bound, and suddenly she felt a great blow to the back of her head as the world burst forth in a kaleidoscope of colors.

CHAPTER THIRTEEN

▼

The sun rose swiftly on the horizon, and a beam slanted into Ian's eyes, awakening him. He yawned and stretched, turning over to avoid its piercing light. When he did, he came into contact with Nikki. When Ian pushed him over slightly, Nikki muttered, "Tiggy, are you finally back? I've been waiting forever."

"Huh?" came Ian's reply as he sat up and rubbed the sleep from his eyes. "What are you murmuring about, Nikki?"

Opening one eye, he replied, "Oh, it's just you." He shut it again. "I thought you were Tiggy."

"What do you mean?" asked Ian, now fully awake and alert.

Yawning, he replied, "I guess I fell asleep waiting for Tiggy to come back with Tuthmosis."

Leaning closer to him, Ian declared with such intensity that Nikki opened his eyes and became scared, "What do you mean Tiggy never came back last night?"

"Just that she didn't come back while I was awake. I guess I fell asleep, but the last time I saw her she was with Tuthmosis, standing back there," he said while pointing to the rear of the barge.

Ian jumped to his feet, strode over to her tent, and swept aside the material. "Empty! Just as I thought!" he declared angrily.

Nikki, coming up behind him, asked, "What's wrong, Ian? Is Tiggy not there?"

"No!" he responded angrily.

"Where could she be?" he asked.

"You don't want to know," declared Ian as he stomped off toward the side of the barge.

"What's going on around here?" said Nikki as he watched Ian's retreating back.

Feeling a tap on his shoulder, Nikki turned around to see the princess standing behind him. "Good morning," she stated, but Nikki just stared at her, not understanding. Again, she repeated the phrase, and finally he figured out the word for *morning* in Egyptian. He nodded and smiled, unsure of how to respond. Then he heard her say "Amanda," for it did not translate. He just shook his head and beckoned her to follow him. Upon reaching Tiggy's tent, he swept aside the material, just as Ian had done, revealing that she was not within and that the sheets had not even been mussed. He mimed to her that he had not seen Tiggy since she was with the pharaoh.

Nikki watched as Merira stood there silently for a moment, contemplating what he had been trying to tell her.

Patting Nikki on his shoulder, she waved toward the rest of the barge, indicating that she wanted him to search for Tiggy.

Nikki ran toward Ian, saying, "Merira wants us to look for Tiggy, because she can't find her either."

Without turning toward Nikki, Ian retorted in a harsh voice, "Tell her to go look with Tuthmosis. I'm sure she is with him!"

Nikki stared at him with a confused look for a moment and then demanded, "What's with you? You've been mad at Tiggy about something since last night. What's she ever done to make you mad?" he finished hotly.

Sighing, Ian turned and said, "I'm not mad at her—just mad that she is shutting me out. She has some crazy plan about getting the last piece, but she won't tell me what it is because she knows I'll try and stop her."

"Oh," stated Nikki. Thinking a minute, he then stated, "Tiggy did tell me that she has to get the final piece. She said the inscription was extremely clear on who had to give it to her. I remember that she wasn't happy about it. But she wouldn't tell me either, so don't feel left out. We both know Tiggy better than that; she won't tell you a thing if she thinks she's protecting you."

"I thought it was the other way around: we're supposed to protect her. Isn't that what the inscription on the top of the chest of the auta said and also what Merira told us?"

As if his words had conjured her up, Merira appeared, looking very agitated. She spoke very quickly and gestured with her hands and arms. Nikki and Ian looked at one another in confusion, not understanding what she was trying to say to them. Finally, over and over again, she said, "Amanda."

"I think, Nikki, that she is trying to tell us something about Tiggy," declared Ian finally. "Let's check the barge for her, even if we have to disturb Tuthmosis to find her."

"Uh," said Nikki with a worried look, "I'll just let you look for her there."

Quickly, the three spread out across the barge, looking for Tiggy in everyone's tent. When Ian glanced into the pharaoh's tent, he felt for sure that he would see her there. However, all he found was Tuthmosis, who looked very angry at the intrusion. Bowing, Ian stated, "I am looking for Princess Amanda." He knew that Tuthmosis could not understand the words he was saying, but he knew that he would understand "Amanda."

Ian was right, for when Tuthmosis heard "Amanda," the angry expression left his face and was replaced by one of curiosity.

Moments later, Tuthmosis emerged, his eyes searching for Princess Amanda, her centurion, or her slave. Quickly, he spied her two attendants going from tent to tent. Seeing Princess Merira, he walked over to her.

"What is going on this morning with Princess Amanda that her centurion would interrupt me?"

"It seems that Princess Amanda is not to be found," returned Merira with concern.

"What!" he exclaimed. "Not to be found? She was still on board when I left her at the rear of the barge last night." Quickly, he strode across the deck toward where they had stood last evening. Mounting the steps, he quickly spied the thin piece of gauze that she had been wearing in her hair last night. Grasping it to him, he turned to see Ian standing behind him. Thrusting it out, Ian took hold of it.

Instantly, he recognized it as the long blue scarf that he had given to Tiggy when he had returned from a trip to China. He pointed to it, saying to Tuthmosis, "Princess Amanda's," and then pointed to his hair to indicate that she had worn it yesterday.

Tuthmosis nodded his understanding but was confused as to where she could be.

Nikki breathlessly mounted the steps toward them, loudly declaring, "Ian, Tiggy's not on this boat. I'm scared! What could've happened to her? Do you think she fell overboard or went back to our time?"

"No, if she fell overboard, someone would have heard her scream, and she couldn't go back, because she doesn't have all the pieces."

Ian began to pace while trying to think.

"Ian, what are we going to do?" demanded Nikki as he grabbed on to his arm.

Stopping, Ian placed his hand on Nikki's shoulder and said, "I don't know, Nikki. Just let me think this thing through. We'll find her, I am sure!"

Tuthmosis watched as Princess Amanda's centurion and slave talked, and he was certain that they had no knowledge of her whereabouts. He could see the fear on the young boy's face and the worried eyes of her warrior.

Turning, Tuthmosis commanded his magi to scour the barge for any missing person or persons and for anything else that looked out of the ordinary.

Princess Merira came to his side, asking, "What is it? Have you found Princess Amanda?"

"She is not on board, and I found her headdress lying on the wood where she was standing when I left her last night."

"I do not understand. Where could she go?" questioned Princess Merira.

"I do not think that she willingly left. There have been many attempts on her life, and I fear that she was taken from this spot."

"Taken? By whom?" said Merira. "She knows no one here except for me. Who would want to do her harm?"

"Hessam tried twice to kill her," supplied the pharaoh.

"Yes, but why?" countered Merira.

"Of this I do not know, but when we reach Cairo, we will turn the barge around and head back toward Deir-el-Bahari and see if he has some answers for me!" demanded Tuthmosis as he slammed his fist into his palm. "Until then, we must keep her centurion and slave calm, for the festival must not be disturbed for our people."

"Yes, Pharaoh," said Merira quietly as she turned to talk to Nikki and Ian.

Meanwhile, far away from the royal barge, Tiggy was awakened by a throbbing headache in a cool, dark room. She was still bound, but she had been laid on some kind of cot. Vague memories floated through her aching head as she tried to sit up. She had no idea where she was or who had taken her. The men's faces had been completely covered with black cloth, with only their eyes showing. She had been terrified and was even more so as she realized that no one had any idea where she had gone or what had happened.

Suddenly, she was alerted to a noise coming from outside the room where she was being kept. She could discern a small ray of light, from a flickering flame, coming in through a crack in the door. Closing her eyes, she lay absolutely still. She heard the creaking of the door as well as several voices as the light from a torch filled the room. She could feel the heat from the flame as they brought the light near her face.

She heard one of the men say, "You have not killed her, have you?"

"No," came the reply. "I must have hit her harder than I intended. Come … let us untie her and bring her forth. The movement of being carried might awaken her."

Tiggy felt gentle hands lifting her and bearing her up what she assumed to be stairs. The sounds and sensations of the outside world greeted her: birds singing, the wind on her cheeks, the warmth of the sun, and the groan of a camel in protest. As gently as she had been picked up, she was laid down upon some silken cushions. She lay there, not moving, trying to regulate her breathing despite the racing of her heart, for she knew that she was not alone.

Soon a voice reached her ears, deep and resonant: "The pharaoh is wise to wish to possess someone so beautiful and unique. Her hair rivals the beauty of the morning sun."

Tiggy felt fingers touch her hair as the voice continued: "How hard did you hit her for her to remain asleep for so long a time?"

"Harder than I thought, o mighty one," came the hesitant reply.

"Leave us. I will wait for her to awaken," came the deep voice again.

Despite her fears, the voice had a soothing effect on her, and because she was weary from the previous day's activities, she dropped off into an unexpected slumber.

Settling himself comfortably in the chair, the man waited for her to awaken.

The sun was high in the morning sky when she finally stirred and opened her eyes to see an old man watching her intently. For a man nearing what she believed to be seventy, he was handsome, with pleasantly chiseled features and with few lines upon his face. His eyes were gentle yet held a look of strength. She felt no fear, and she assumed from his look that he was sizing her up. Conscious of her still throbbing head, she cautiously swung her legs to the side of the divan upon which she lay and slowly sat up. Looking around, she noticed that she was on a covered patio of sorts, which appeared to be attached to a private home far from the noise of the city.

Silence reigned as they looked at each other across the few feet that separated them. She waited for the man to speak. She knew that she needed to keep her wits about her and not antagonize the man. Based on his clothing and bearing, she gathered that he was a man of culture and wealth. She would wait to see what he wanted with her, for patience not only was a virtue but also could save her life.

Still at ease in his chair, the man finally spoke: "You are a stranger in a strange land, and you are wondering why I have taken you away from the pharaoh."

Tiggy simply nodded her head.

"You are wise enough to be silent and listen?" he questioned as he leaned forward, now alert to the presence of even the wind.

Again, she nodded, thinking that this man was very shrewd. Steeling herself so as not to betray a single emotion, she felt prepared to meet any question that he could possibly ask her.

"Good," he agreed. Leaning back in his chair, he declared, "You have great wisdom for one who is so young."

Tiggy said nothing.

He laughed aloud and then nodded his approval. "Hatshepsut failed to tell me that the vision would be as wise as she is beautiful."

Tiggy arched an eyebrow in silent question to his statement.

Again he laughed. "You are a shrewd one."

Funny, she thought. *I was thinking the same thing about you.*

"I know that you seek the wealth of the Pharaoh Hatshepsut," he simply stated while toying with a wine goblet. Yet his eyes missed nothing.

Not a flicker of emotion or a glimmer in her eyes betrayed Tiggy's thoughts. She was in complete control of her facial expression to show no knowledge or emotion. *If he thinks I am that easy to read, then he is in for a surprise.*

Nodding his head again, he looked at her with admiration. "I know more about the dream than anyone," he declared. Leaning forward, he said eagerly, "I know how you can gain the final piece that you seek, for I know that you have the ankh."

She remained expressionless, yet her body was tense.

For several minutes, she endured this man's questions and gleaned all sorts of useful information. However, more than just a treasure was at stake; her life as well as the lives of Ian and Nikki hung in the balance, and she dared not reveal any of what she knew.

So in silence she sat.

She has courage! he thought. *Now let us see how long you will keep this secret when confronted with physical pain.* Snapping his fingers, he signaled to the men dressed in black to take hold of her. *Forgive me, Hatshepsut, for I know this is not what you wished. But I need to see how far she will go and what she will endure to remain true to your secret.*

She had expected him first to try to persuade her verbally, and now she figured that she would have to endure physical torture. Suddenly the vision that she had seen while holding the lotus flower to the column flashed through her mind. Now she realized that the vision was about to come true, and she prepared herself to endure the torture she feared was to come. Therefore, she knew they were surprised when she did not resist.

Two men in black quickly tied her up and made her face a stone wall not far away from where she had sat. Fear raced through her veins, and her heart pounded as she wondered what they were about to do to her. She had never been subjected to violence and was horrified at the idea that she was about to be tortured. However, she knew that she must remain strong for the sake of the others. At the first lash, she saw black but refused to allow herself to faint. She also refused to cry out, so she bit her lip instead. After four lashes, the same men untied her. She felt faint and sank to the ground.

Picking her up, one of the men carried her toward a table covered with knives. They sat her in a chair nearby and proceeded to tie her to it. She watched the sun glisten on the blade of a long wicked-looking knife. Swallowing hard, she turned her head away as it approached.

Shaking her head, Tiggy finally shouted, "No! Stop this!" Struggling, she tried to free herself, but her efforts were futile.

Strong fingers dug into the top of her shoulders. Tiggy started to shake as she watched the sharp point come closer. Slowly, the man pulled the knife down her left hand. The sound of her scream could be heard for miles in the stillness of the late morning. As the man drew the knife down her arm again, she promptly fainted.

"Untie her," demanded the man who had ordered her to be tortured.

A second man standing nearby declared, "She is the chosen one! Pharaoh Hatshepsut said that she would have courage greater than that of any man."

Nodding his head in agreement, the older man told them to return her to the divan.

An hour later, Tiggy awoke to find the same man sitting in the same chair and looking at her in the same way; this time, however, sadness filled his eyes. *Did I dream the whole thing?* she wondered. *No, for my body is in terrible pain.*

Seeing her awake, the man quickly drew his chair closer to where she lay. "Forgive me for what I have done to you. Know this: it was necessary to prove to me and my men that you would keep the promise of Pharaoh Hatshepsut safe."

Tiggy blinked her eyes as if to focus. She thought that she had not clearly understood what the man had said. Confusion reigned on her face, and the man saw it immediately.

"Let me tell you who I am, and then maybe you will trust me. My name is Senenmut."

At his words, Tiggy did not control her emotions. She instantly sat up, only to fall back down, weak with pain.

"I see from your response that you know who I am," he responded.

"Yes, I do," said Tiggy, finding her voice at last.

"You are the chosen one," he said, "for your voice is as soft and melodious as the whispering wind or the song of the seas. This was also foretold."

"You are Senenmut?" she questioned in disbelief. "You were to have disappeared when Pharaoh Hatshepsut disappeared."

"And so I did and will," he agreed.

"But Princess Merira misses you terribly. It has been hard enough with her mother gone, but your absence has also affected her greatly."

"For this, I am sorry," he said with a sigh. "But she has chosen to align herself with Tuthmosis as his God Wife. You must know that she knows of you and what your journey here is for."

"Yes, she knows!" declared Tiggy. "She has helped us greatly."

Sitting quietly for a moment, lost in thought, he then said, "Do you remember the warning in the wind?"

Her eyes widened in response to this question. "Yes, I do. It said to beware of many and trust few."

Nodding his head, he responded, "Yes, trust few!"

Then he hesitated, and Tiggy sensed he was withholding something from her. Abruptly, he changed the subject back to why she had been abducted from the royal barge.

"I had to be sure that you were in fact the one chosen, the one to come and protect Pharaoh Hatshepsut's wealth from those who wish to destroy it. You have proven yourself to have the courage that she foretold you would have. I am sorry to have wounded you, for I know that it was painful," he said with remorse. "Time will heal your wounds, but it will not heal the sadness in my heart for the death of the one I love greatly."

Reaching out her hand, Tiggy placed it over his. "I am sorry for your loss. I can imagine that you love her still."

"Yes," he continued sadly, "I will for eternity." Sighing, he said, "But death is coming swiftly for me. I know that my time is short, and I will be with her in the afterlife. But before I go, I promised myself that I would speak with you."

Senenmut grasped her hand tightly, begging her with his eyes to listen to him. "You must allow Hatshepsut to live on through the centuries. Do not allow her memory to be destroyed, as I have seen her cartouche being chiseled off her buildings, obelisks, temples, and everything else she has created."

"That you have created," corrected Tiggy.

"Yes, things I created for her out of love, not out of lust for power or wealth," he agreed.

"I will not be able to stop Tuthmosis from chiseling off her cartouches, for it has already begun to be done in great numbers," said Tiggy with the utmost frankness.

"Yes, of this I know!" cried Senenmut. "But there is a great treasure that will speak of her reign and her life. It will live through you and your children's children. We will both live on if you find her wealth and display it and her power to the world. Promise me you will do this," again begged the desperate man before her.

Searching his eyes, she saw the pleading within them. She knew that he needed to hear her promise before he died. "Yes, I promise to find and tell the world about the great and strong rule of Pharaoh Hatshepsut."

Tears coursed down his cheeks at her words, and then he quietly muttered, "Then I can leave this world and go to be with her."

Minutes ticked by as the old man wept with his coming joy and his present grief. Then, coming to his senses, he declared with renewed vigor, "My magi will bring you a jeweled bracelet made of lotus flowers to wear around your wrist. It will appear in your room, and you are to wear it only when you have been given the last piece by Tuthmosis."

Tiggy nodded her head in understanding.

Leaning forward, he continued feverishly, "Wear it as soon as you get the piece from Tuthmosis! Not a minute a later."

Tiggy leaned back against the divan. Her thoughts and emotions were in turmoil. This adventure had become even more complicated and more dangerous than she could have ever imagined.

Senenmut continued, "My men will bring all of you to a special room hidden in the palace known only to myself and Hatshepsut. There, you and your attendants will join the pieces and travel back to your own time. The pieces will then show you the way."

After sitting thoughtfully for a moment, Tiggy asked, "But when we join the pieces together, in our own time, won't we just come back here?"

"No, for I hold the lock to keep you or anyone else from coming back here again."

She looked up in surprise as he held out two elongated and thin rounded pieces of gold that formed a cross about six inches long from a golden chain he wore around his neck.

"Taking them apart into two pieces," he declared, "you put the pieces together. You must slide them through these and lock the ends when all the pieces are together. This will allow you to be transported back to the very day you left, and it will also allow you to use the map to find the treasure," he said in hushed tones. "I am sure that you have realized already that the pieces, once joined together, create the map," he added, almost as an afterthought.

Tiggy nodded. "Yes, I realized that when I found the second piece. I have to ask you, though, what do I do with this?" She drew forth from her clothes the amulet.

"You are the one!" he cried. At her questioning look, he clarified his statement. "It is written that the chosen one is the only person to whom the amulet will come off of the chest of the auta. A curse was placed on it to prevent others from removing it. It is written that only the one from the vision, the one who is pure in heart and spirit, will be allowed to touch the amulet and remove it successfully. Others may put the map together, but only one, the one who holds the power of the sun in her hand, may open the chamber."

Tiggy sat back, dumbfounded at what Senenmut had imparted. Interrupting her thoughts, he continued, "Even I am unsure of how you must use the amulet, but you will surely know once you have arrived at your journey's end."

She leaned back against the divan to assimilate what she had been told. Her back smarted and began to throb, and Senenmut felt guilty as he saw her wince in pain. Expressing his thoughts aloud, he said, "Again, pardon me for having inflicted pain upon you."

"I understand why," she responded quietly. "If you could treat or wrap my wounds, then I believe they will begin to heal properly."

She stared at him in disbelief as he shook his head. "No, I will return you to the pharaoh's house the way you are."

"Why?"

"You have been abducted from the royal barge and have been injured. Your story will be more credible if you return to the royal house injured and bound as a prisoner. No, you will be returned as you are with a letter of warning about foreigners or some such nonsense. You will remember nothing from this event, only a darkened room and torture."

Tiggy nodded at the wisdom of his words. Laying her hand upon his arm, she said quietly, "I will try to do what is right for you and Hatshepsut. I will always remember you and what you have achieved and the great love you had for her. You will live on—I promise you that."

The tears welled up in his eyes as well as in her eyes as he grasped her hands in his. A silent bond was formed, and a sacred promise was enacted, each knowing the enormity of the task before them and pledging to do what they knew to be right. Then, as one of his magi walked up, he nodded his head, stating simply, "Come … it is time. Darkness is creeping upon us, and I wish to return you under the cover of night." Handing her a goblet, he said, "Drink this, for it will make you sleep for many hours past your arrival at the palace. Thank you and farewell, for we will not meet again."

On an impulse, she reached out and embraced Senenmut quickly. Then, slowly, she drank the sweet liquid and marveled at how rapidly her vision began to blur and darkness swallowed her.

CHAPTER FOURTEEN

▼

Miles away at Deir el-Bahri, several anxious people paced the confines of their rooms, each having the same thoughts: *Where could she be? And who could have taken her?*

Nikki watched in wonder as Ian restlessly paced back and forth across the room that had been allotted to them. "I can't believe that I was so stupid, so stubborn, to have let my anger get in the way. If I would've been more watchful, I could've saved Tiggy from being abducted," Ian said for what Nikki thought had been the millionth time during the course of the day.

"Ian," he returned as he looked out over the balcony, "there's no way you could've had any idea that this was going to happen. We've been over this before about a million times," he muttered under his breath.

"Nikki, don't mutter. It's annoying! Just say what you're going to say and get it over with, will you?" replied a stressed and frustrated Ian.

"I just think we need to be looking for her, not just sitting around waiting for her to come back or for some dumb ransom note to be brought. I mean, come on—that's not going to happen! We need to look for her!"

"Yes, I agree," said Ian as he stopped pacing. "But where? I don't have a clue what to do or who would've taken her. I would start with Hessam, but I think Tuthmosis has already done that." Ian sank down on a nearby couch, running his fingers through his hair in frustration at the situation before him. Never had he been so confounded; he had always been able to think of a solution or fix a problem. Now, with such a crucial situation before him, he could not find a solution.

Leaning back against the cushions, he said, "Think, Ian … think. You must be missing something."

Nikki, tired of his frustrations, stepped onto the balcony that overlooked the most distant part of the gardens. He too had been trying to remember everything that Tiggy had said, any clue she might have given, but he too drew a complete blank. As he watched the torches that illuminated the garden dance in the night breeze, a movement caught his attention. Narrowing his eyes, he tried to locate its source. He saw several men creeping through the plants. His eyes grew wide as he saw the glint of a sword at the waist of one of the men. Leaning over the railing, he tried harder to see what they were carrying. He thought it odd that anyone would be doing anything in the garden at this time of night, and the clothes the men wore were different from anything he had seen at the palace.

Quietly, Nikki went back inside the room and called for Ian. "Ian, come here," he whispered, waving his hand. "Come look at this."

Rising to his feet, Ian was alerted to the tenseness in Nikki's voice. "What is it?"

"Shh … be quiet. I don't want them to hear us or know that we are watching."

"Who?" asked Ian as he joined Nikki on the balcony.

"Them," he declared as he pointed out across the garden.

"What is that they have?"

"I have no idea," whispered Nikki. "That's why I asked you to look."

They watched for another minute before they saw the men turn and quickly flee the garden. The wind suddenly blew, and a sudden bolt of lightning lit the sky, causing both to jump. The lightning flashed again as Ian strained his eyes to see what the men had placed in the garden.

As the wind blew harder, the veil that had been placed over Tiggy's face was lifted by the wind; and with the next lightning flash, both Ian and Nikki gasped as they saw her face as she lay in the garden were the men had placed her.

Instantly, both turned and fled back into the room, intent on reaching her as quickly as possible. The bang of the room doors, as they ran through, echoed down the corridors. Racing by slaves and magi, they did not stop to tell anyone of their discovery. Several of the magi followed, and one went to inform Tuthmosis that the foreigners were seen running from their rooms toward the gardens.

Within minutes, they reached her side. Ian placed a finger on the side of her neck, searching for a pulse. He bent his head and said a prayer of thanksgiving as he felt a slow but steady pulse. Turning to Nikki, he quietly stated, "She is alive."

Expelling the breath that he did not realize he had been holding, Nikki sank down onto the grass.

Ian tried to awaken her by calling and shaking her softly. As the lightning flashed again, Nikki said, "Let's get her inside before the storm hits."

Ian was bending down to gather her up into his arms when a group of people came rushing into the garden. Tuthmosis, wearing a grave expression, was at the front of this group. "Is she dead?" he demanded.

But neither Ian nor Nikki understood him. Ian just picked her up and carried her past them into the palace. The pharaoh and his magi could only follow. The journey back to their rooms took much longer than the journey to the garden, and in the light of the corridors, all could see that Tiggy was bleeding onto the marble floors.

Nikki swiftly ran ahead to open the doors for Ian as they approached. Crossing the room, Ian went to the bedroom and laid Tiggy upon the bed. It was then that Nikki saw the note attached to the rope that bound her.

Tuthmosis entered the room just as Nikki held up the note for Ian to see. Pausing, he held out the note to the pharaoh, knowing that Tuthmosis could read it whereas he could not.

Ian was completely oblivious to anything other than his attempts to awaken Tiggy. While he was placing a cool linen cloth to her forehead, Nikki took out a knife and cut the cord that was binding her hands and feet. Both Nikki and Ian started when Tuthmosis shouted something in fury.

"They will surely die for this!" he roared as he looked about at his magi. "Now, search the area for anyone who does not belong. Find them who did this to her or take her place."

The magi bowed and quickly left the room, fearful of the pharaoh's anger.

Princess Merira entered the room as the magi were leaving, declaring loudly, "You have found her? Is she alive? Who took her?"

"We know nothing except that she was in the garden."

Nikki stepped back from the bed as Tuthmosis came nearer. Sitting down on the side of the bed, he picked up Tiggy's left arm, which was bleeding onto the floor. Quickly, he gave orders for servants to attend her and priests to bind her wounds. Ian put his arm beneath her shoulders, lifted her up slightly, and poured a few drops of water into her mouth; however, the water ran down her cheek, and he laid her back down upon the pillow. Merira gasped and pointed to his arm, for it had come away with blood upon it. Gently, Ian sat her back up, and all could see that her garment was torn and that blood was seeping through the wounds that had been inflicted upon her back.

Merira began to cry, mumbling, "Why? Why?" over and over again.

Tears welled up in Nikki's eyes, because he felt guilty at wanting this whole adventure in the first place.

"My god in heaven!" exclaimed Ian in hot anger. "Who could have done this to her?" Looking up, he met the eyes of Tuthmosis, whose anger mirrored his own. They looked at each other questioningly, each searching the eyes of the other as if to find answers there.

Soon handmaidens and priests entered the room, bearing ointment and linen bandages to attend to her wounds.

Ian, knowing that they would soon be unclothing Tiggy, knew that he must obtain the pieces from her before they were discovered. "Nikki, we need to get everyone out of the room so I can get Tiggy's pieces. Quick—make some kind of distraction."

Nikki immediately pointed toward the balcony and began to run; instantly all followed, except Ian. Knowing he did not have much time, he bent down and grasped all the chains he could feel on Tiggy's neck. Quickly, he took the chains off and placed them around his own neck, tucking them inside his clothes. When everyone returned, they saw Ian wiping her face.

Glancing around to see if anyone else was in the room, Tuthmosis signaled a magi to send in the priests to attend Tiggy. Ian stood up and stepped back as Merira quickly shooed everyone out of the room.

Nikki and Ian were surprised when Tuthmosis sat down upon the couch as if to wait. Seeing that there was nothing that they could do, they sat down on a couch across from him. Nikki looked from one worried face to the other. He silently agreed with himself that Tuthmosis had nothing to do with Tiggy's abduction, but that left him with two problems: one, who did hurt Tiggy, and second, whoever did was still on the loose.

Several minutes later, Princess Merira emerged from Tiggy's room.

Ian and Nikki watched as the pharaoh shouted and paced the room, ranting and pounding his fist into his hand after every strange sentence Merira uttered. Ian and Nikki looked at each other, and finally Ian asked, "Do you understand anything that he's saying?"

"Some words, but not enough to make any sense out of it."

"This is just great!" said Ian. "We're stuck in another time around people whom we don't understand, and the only person who knows how to get us out of this mess is lying unconscious in the other room."

Nikki nodded as he now watched both Ian and Tuthmosis pace back and forth across the room. "Kind of stinks, doesn't it?" said Nikki as he looked at Merira and shrugged his shoulders.

For several hours, Nikki and Merira watched and endured the two men as they went from fits of anger to fits of dismay. Finally, the door to Tiggy's room opened, and a handmaiden appeared. She bowed to the pharaoh and said, "O mighty one of Amun-Ra, the lady is stirring."

At her words, both Tuthmosis and Merira hurried toward her room, leaving Ian and Nikki to follow. Tuthmosis went to her side and sat in a chair that had been drawn up next to the bed. Merira and Nikki stood at her feet while Ian knelt on the other side of the bed from Tuthmosis. They watched for several minutes with bated breath for Tiggy to open her eyes. Finally, after what seemed like an eternity, she said softly, "Ian? Nikki?"

Tuthmosis grabbed her hand while Ian bent close to her face. For Tiggy, it seemed that she was swimming through a dark river and was trying to surface. She could see a light, but it seemed far off in the distance. She tried going toward it with all of her might, and the nearer she came, the more she could hear. She surfaced with a gasp, for it seemed as if she had been underwater too long.

She sat up suddenly, and gentle hands laid her back down. Finally, her eyes took on a more intelligent look and could focus on those around her. Breathing out, she said, turning to look at Ian, "Did I dream it all? Was that all it was? A bad dream?"

Shaking his head sadly, he stated, "No, it wasn't a dream." A tear slipped down his cheek, and she asked, "What is it?"

"I thought I had lost you. I thought that you had been murdered!"

"No," she said distantly, "I'll be all right. I only feel this way from the drug that they gave me."

"Drug?" asked Nikki in surprise. "You knew these people who abducted you gave you a drug?"

"Yes," she replied simply.

"Can you talk to us? Can you tell us anything?" asked Ian in earnest.

Shaking her head as if to clear it, Tiggy responded, "Yes, but not now, because your face will give it away. Wait until they have gone, and I'll tell you everything that happened."

Nodding his head, Ian sat back and allowed Tiggy to talk with Tuthmosis and Merira.

Turning her head, she glanced at Tuthmosis and said weakly, "Pharaoh, please protect me! Do not allow me to come to harm again."

"No one will touch you! I will protect you from now on. You will be in my care alone!" he said as he reached out and touched her cheek. "I am sorry that you have been so treacherously treated while in my kingdom. I will seek out the malefactors and kill them myself to avenge your blood which has been spilled upon this soil."

Reaching out her bandaged arm, she touched his and said gently, "Please, just keep me safe. Never have I known violence or been treated so horribly. I'm frightened, sire," she continued, her eyes begging him to keep her safe.

Tuthmosis was moved by her plea and gently said, "I have given you my word, Princess, and I *will* guard you."

"Thank you, sire," she said.

Letting out a deep sigh, she softly continued, "I can rest now, knowing that you will keep me safe."

As her eyelids started to close, Tuthmosis asked urgently, "Can you tell me anything? Who did this or how this happened?"

Opening her eyes slightly, she said, "I don't know who did this. I heard voices but saw no faces. They had me in a cool and dark room where I couldn't feel the warmth of the sun." Tiggy shivered at her remembrance.

Tuthmosis took note and placed a gentle hand on her arm. "It is too painful for you?" he questioned.

"Yes," she replied very softly. "I have never known such violence." A small tear ran down the corner of her cheek as she closed her eyes and turned her head away.

Reaching out, he wiped the tear and asked, "How did you leave the royal barge?"

Looking up to meet his eyes, she began to blush a bright red as she remembered what had occurred right before she was taken.

"What is it?" he asked as he saw her hesitation.

"I finally got up and looked out over the water to watch the moon shining upon its surface. I remember thinking that it was a lovely sight," she said quietly. "When I turned to go, I heard a noise at the back of the barge which seemed to be coming from the water. So, I went back to where I was standing and bent over to see what had made the noise. I saw a boat tied there and thought that it was odd, but since I saw no one, I just decided to leave."

Then she gave a great shutter, and he tightened his hand on hers as if to give her strength. "When I stood back up from leaning over the railing, I felt a hand slip over my mouth and a knife press against my throat," she said as her voice cracked with emotion. With wide eyes, she reached up and touched her throat as she shuddered.

They all could see a red line at the base of her throat where the skin had been cut by the pressure of the knife.

She continued, "I then felt a great blow to the back of my head and knew nothing until I awakened bound on a cot in a cool, dark room."

Silence reigned in the room. Merira finally broke the silence. "Come," she said as she straightened the blanket around Tiggy. "You have been through a terrifying ordeal and need your rest."

Tuthmosis nodded his head. "Yes, you need to rest. We will speak of this tomorrow if you are strong enough to talk about that which occurred."

Sighing deeply, she closed her eyes and pretended to drift off to sleep. One by one, they left her room, and she heard the pharaoh giving orders for the magi to surround her room inside and outside.

After a few moments, she heard Ian say, "They've all gone now. You can open your eyes."

When she did, Tiggy smiled, asking, "How did you know?"

"I just know you," he returned as he smiled down at her. "So, do you think that you can tell me what happened?"

"Yes, I need to actually. It's important that you and Nikki know what's happening."

"I agree!"

Slowly, she let out a breath and began. "I am going to give you the abbreviated version, just in case they return."

In a low voice, she informed Ian what had occurred after she had been taken from the royal barge. As Tiggy described her torture, she paused to catch her breath as she remembered the pain she had endured. Shaking her head, she continued on to the most crucial part. She told Ian how it was Senenmut who had tortured her and why.

"Senenmut?" cried Ian in disbelief. "I thought he disappeared with Hatshepsut."

"He did!" she confirmed. "However, he did not die as everyone believes but remained alive, waiting for us, me in particular, to come. He also told me an enormous amount about the last pieces and about how to join them, and he gave me the 'locks' to the map that will prevent anyone from following us back to our own time." She felt around her neck for the chains and exclaimed excitedly, "They're gone!"

"No, not gone," said Ian as he drew forth the chains he had taken from her.

"Thank you, God," she said with relief. When she sat up, Ian reached out and fastened the chains around her neck. Quickly, she placed the small pouch containing the pieces, the amulet, and the locks that Senenmut had given her back inside her clothing.

Settling back down, Ian asked, "But how do you know that you can trust him? I mean, he tortured you, for heaven's sake!" he exclaimed with renewed anger.

"I can't explain it, Ian. You just had to be there and see his face and look into his eyes. Senenmut thinks that because this has happened to me, the pharaoh will be more than willing to give me the piece. Remember, Tuthmosis has no idea what the piece really means. To him, it is the goddess of protection—that is all."

"Hmm," said Ian, thinking. "He just might be right. You know, Tiggy, I don't think Tuthmosis is really that bad of an individual. He has some problems, to be sure, but he certainly is not as evil as history has portrayed him."

"I agree," said Tiggy. "I think that he is embarrassed that a woman ruled Egypt and is trying to act like it never happened by eradicating anything that could prove her existence. I feel that Merira is the one who 'helped' her mother disappear."

"If I were a betting man, I would say that Hessam killed Hatshepsut and that this is the secret of Merira's that he holds."

"Could be, Ian. I never thought about it that way. Anyway, it is imperative that you and Nikki be with me at all times once I leave Tuthmosis's presence with the last piece."

"I wholeheartedly agree. It is time for this adventure to come to a close. Know this, though, Tiggy: once you have the piece, we will not leave your side except for the most personal of reasons!" Swallowing hard, he continued in a quavering voice, "I almost lost you once, and I refuse to ever be in that situation again."

Bending down, he placed a kiss upon her cheek. "Sleep well."

Tiggy lay on her bed, stunned, and watched him through her lashes as he went across the room and lay down upon her couch. She detected an air of finality about him that she dared not question. She accepted it for what it was—his protection. It was obvious that Ian had no intention of letting her out of his sight. Sighing deeply, she closed her eyes and swiftly fell into a deep slumber.

CHAPTER FIFTEEN

▼

At midday, Nikki awoke first and walked in between the magi that were surrounding Tiggy's room. Cautiously, he opened the door and saw that Ian and Tiggy were still sound asleep. Closing it carefully, he went to seek out some food, for he was powerfully hungry. Nikki glanced around to see that Tuthmosis was good to his word, because never had he seen so many guards walking around the gardens and the palace. It seemed as if their numbers had tripled since last night.

"Well, we should be safe," he mused as he wandered into the room where food was laid out upon the tables. Slowly looking over the great pile of fruits, fish, and wild game, he noticed Merira walking toward him with Tuthmosis. He bowed at their arrival and quickly stepped away from the table.

Merira reached out and said something to him, but he did not understand until he heard her say "Amanda." Then he mimed that she was still fast asleep. Nodding her head, Merira walked toward the table at which Tuthmosis now sat.

Nikki stared at the food while trying to listen to their conversation. He couldn't understand all of what they said, but he hoped that he could pick out a few words that would let him know what they were thinking.

Sitting down, Merira watched Tuthmosis carefully, unsure of what to say or do, for he wore a ferocious look upon his face. Finally, after several minutes, she decided to talk about Tiggy; she didn't really want to, but she felt that she needed to see what he was thinking about doing.

"I am glad that Princess Amanda has returned to us," she said simply. "I was in great fear for her," she continued as she watched his face.

"Yes, I too am glad that she has returned."

"Do you think that I should go and speak to her about what occurred?" she questioned.

"No, I will speak with her," he commanded, "and I will deal with the situation. I want no interference from anyone."

Nikki glanced up from the plate he was slowly filling at the loud sound of Tuthmosis's voice. Seeing the furious look the pharaoh directed toward Merira, Nikki knew that he was right in believing that maybe she was not to be trusted after all.

Merira looked up suddenly, stunned at his harsh tone. "If that is your wish," she replied humbly, "but she is my friend. I would like to know what happened to her."

"No! I forbid anyone other than her centurions to talk with her," he retorted coldly.

"But—," began Merira.

"Cease!" he roared. "I am Pharaoh, and I have spoken! Do not forget your place, woman, and challenge my words!" Tuthmosis banged his fist upon the table and rose to his feet.

Seeing this new development, Nikki quickly filled the remaining plates and left to return to their rooms, eager to tell Ian and Tiggy what he'd witnessed.

When Tuthmosis shouted at Merira, Ian and Tiggy were walking into the garden. Even in the distance, they could hear his shouts.

Tiggy told Ian, "Something is occurring, because Tuthmosis just shouted at someone—I suspect Merira—not to challenge his words!"

Slowing their pace, Tiggy leaned more heavily on Ian for support, trying to appear even weaker as Tuthmosis saw them walking across the garden toward him.

Quickly, Tuthmosis crossed the distance between them.

"Good morning, my fair and beautiful lady," he exclaimed loudly, causing Nikki to look up from the far side of the garden. Seeing Ian and Tiggy, he too crossed the garden and headed in their direction. He felt a sudden urge to tell both of them what he had witnessed.

As the pharaoh came closer, Tiggy, holding on to Ian's arm, curtsied while Ian bowed.

"Good morning, sire," she stated weakly.

"You are feeling well?"

"Yes, sire, I feel better than last night."

Seeing that she held on to Ian for support, he offered his arm instead. "Come ... you are still weak from what has happened. Let us break your fast and eat."

"Thank you, sire," she responded with a shy smile. Walking toward where Merira was eating, Tiggy suddenly asked, "Could we not eat outside,

Pharaoh? The day is lovely, and the warmth of the sun is refreshing after the cold of yesterday." She shivered slightly, which Tuthmosis felt.

"If that is your wish, let it be so," he declared as he waved toward his magi, who were never far from his side. "Bring us food by the bathing pool, and take the centurion with you, for he alone will get the food for the princess."

"That's not necessary, sire," Tiggy pointed out as she saw Nikki crossing the garden toward them. "I see that my slave is already attending to my needs."

She waved at Nikki to come toward her, and she and the pharaoh continued their way toward some chairs next to the bathing pool.

When Nikki came closer, she could tell by the expression on his face that he had something to say. Turning from the pharaoh, she told Ian, "See what Nikki has to say. I think it's important."

But Nikki did not wait to talk to Ian alone. He started talking as soon as he was within hearing distance. "Tiggy, Ian," he burst forth excitedly. "I heard and saw the two of them arguing about something. I think it was about you, Tiggy. I think we need to watch her, because I don't think she's our friend after all."

"I believe you're right, Nikki," said Tiggy with a nod. "But for now, go tell Ian, and leave me alone with Tuthmosis. I need to get that final piece from him."

Both Ian and Nikki nodded as they bowed and walked a few yards away—far enough not to hear them yet close enough to respond if needed.

Turning back toward Tuthmosis, Tiggy said, "Forgive me, Pharaoh, for my slave had something to tell me."

Smiling, he nodded his head in acknowledgment of her apology. Then Tuthmosis felt her hand shaking where he had placed it on his arm. "You are cold?"

"No, sire," she whispered in return. "I am frightened! I've tried not to be, but every time I look at these," she said, pointing to her arm and hand, "I am."

Setting her down in a comfortable chair, Tuthmosis placed a cushion behind her back. "Do not be frightened! I will guard you!"

"That is most gracious of you, Pharaoh, but how can you keep me safe during the night?" she finished with a blush.

"There are ways," he responded gently as he touched her cheek. "I could marry you."

She blushed furiously and looked downward, muttering, "You know that it cannot be so, sire."

Tuthmosis watched as Tiggy delicately tried to cut the meat that Nikki had brought her. Time and time again, she tried to cut it, but putting pressure on her hands brought pain to them. Finally, she put aside her utensils and picked up a piece of fruit.

He stunned Tiggy when he reached out, declaring, "Allow one of my slaves to cut your food for you." Waving his hand, he signaled for one of the slaves standing nearby to do as he bid and cut the food for Tiggy.

"Thank you, for it is difficult for me," she said as she waved her hands in the air.

Once the slave placed the food back before her, she began to eat. Silence reigned in the cloud-covered midday sun. Each contemplated what to say to the other. Tuthmosis finally broke the silence. "Do you think that you can tell me what you remember?"

Immediately she stopped eating, put down the food, and rose to her feet. Walking to the water's edge, she stood, looking downward at the shimmering surface. She started as he touched her elbow, for she had not heard him rise. Looking up, she stated, "I will tell you what I remember."

Pulling her gently back toward the chairs, he remarked, "You must sit and rest, and if the telling becomes too difficult, then you must stop."

Tiggy nodded. Sitting down, she carefully arranged her garments and then began telling her story. "After the blow to the back of my head, I don't remember anything. The first thing that I do remember is waking up in a very dark and cool room. I was tied up and was lying on a bed of some kind, for I remember that it was soft. Soon I heard voices and could see a bit of light streaming in through a crack by the door. Because I was scared, I pretended to be asleep, hoping that they would leave me. Unfortunately, this was not the case. One of the men picked me up and carried me from the room down what I believe were stairs. There, I remember …" Her voice trailed off as she stared into the distance. Her fidgeting hands twisted the cloth into terrible wrinkles. After taking a deep breath, she continued, "The man who was carrying me set me on my feet. When I fell to the ground, someone pulled me up, and I felt my right hand being stretched out and tied. I could feel the coolness of the stone against my cheek, and I dared not open my eyes as they tied my left hand in the same manner." Tiggy paused for dramatic effect.

"Then what?" asked Tuthmosis as he placed his hand over hers.

"I tried to see who was behind me, but the room was not well lit, and the men were draped in black with their faces covered. I spoke to them as I am speaking to you now, but they shouted at me not to speak in a language that was not my own. They shouted again at me for being a stranger in your land. When I tried to speak again, I felt the first lash of a whip," she said as she lowered her voice and a tear ran down her cheek.

Tuthmosis reached out to comfort her, but she checked him by putting up her hand. "Several men then continued shouting at me for being a foreigner and for thinking that I could become the God Wife of the pharaoh; they said I was not fit to be the queen of a people that were not my own. I tried to tell them that I wasn't going to be your wife, but each time I spoke, the man lashed out at me with his whip."

Rising to her feet once again, she moved toward the water's edge. Taking deep breaths, she tried to calm herself, all the while concocting the rest of her story. Tuthmosis came near her but did not touch her. He could see the struggle that was going on within her.

"I feel, sire, that a curse has been put upon me for being here." Pausing, she looked up at the dark gathering clouds.

"That is not true!" he countered.

"I fear that it is, sire. Since my arrival, many terrible things have happened to me. I sense that I must leave this place, for there is evil here that intends to destroy me."

"Come!" he said as he gently reached for her uninjured hand. "I have something that will help protect you."

"May I come with you?" inquired a voice behind them.

Tiggy remained silent as she saw Princess Merira. Tuthmosis replied, "No, we wish to be alone, for the rest of her story needs to be finished. We are retiring to my rooms, for a storm approaches."

Merira's eyes narrowed on Tiggy, and for the first time, Tiggy saw hatred in her eyes. Moving away from Tuthmosis, Tiggy placed a hand on Merira, whispering, "Please know that I would do nothing to ever jeopardize your position with him. He truly only wants to talk to me about what happened. Do not be afraid. I don't want your position."

Merira smiled and kissed her cheek, but Tiggy could see that the smile never reached her eyes and that her show of affection was more theatrical than genuine. Tiggy sensed at that moment that Merira would betray her, Ian, and Nikki. She had a strong feeling that Merira knew too much about her mother's dream, and her urgency to find Hatshepsut's treasure now seemed to make sense. She did not want to protect her mother's wealth or memory; she wanted the gold for reasons of her own. Did she have her mother murdered, Tiggy now wondered, or was it some other person, like the head magi, Hessam?

All these thoughts raced through Tiggy's head as she crossed the garden with Tuthmosis.

"One moment please, sire," declared Tiggy. "I wish to talk to my slave." Looking toward Nikki in the distance, she waved him over. Quickly, he traversed the distance that separated them; bowing, he looked at Tiggy anxiously.

"Where is Ian?" she asked first.

"He said that he was going to pack our things."

"Good," she said with a nod. "Now, go tell him that I am retiring to his rooms"—she looked at Tuthmosis—"and that he will be giving me something. You must have everything ready to go and leave nothing behind. Merira is watching us, so use the utmost caution!"

At his look of comprehension, she questioned, "You suspected that Merira might be the one to watch?"

"Not until this morning," he acknowledged.

"Well, tell Ian what you suspect, and for now, be alert, cautious, and, most of all, careful. Danger is upon us." As he bowed and turned to go, she grasped his arm. "Nikki, I am scared this time. It's not a joke. This could very well mean our lives." Staring at her with wide eyes, he finally bowed and turned to leave.

"The boy was scared," stated Tuthmosis. "What did you say to him?"

"I told him that I was going to your rooms and that I didn't wish to be disturbed. I also told him that I was scared and that I was afraid that the evil here would eventually kill me."

"This will not happen!" declared Tuthmosis as he drew her closer to himself. "I will give you the protection of Amun-Ra and my own as well. You will not perish."

Entering his rooms at last, Tuthmosis demanded that all leave them, even his bodyguards. "I wish to be alone with you," he said as he reached out to run his fingers through her hair. "Come ... sit and finish your story."

"Sire, I am scared," she began as she walked toward the balcony. For a moment, she looked out at the gathering dark clouds. She stayed silent for several moments, allowing herself time to formulate a tentative plan. Turning, she faced him and said, "See? Even the clouds are telling me to beware, that there is evil here. Oh, sire, what am I to do?" A sob escaped her, and she turned fleeing onto the balcony. As she held on to the railing, silent tears began to fall, and she felt raindrops splash upon her hands.

Tuthmosis cautiously came up behind her. Saying nothing, he turned her to face him. Looking down into her tear-streaked face, he said, "Come ... return inside, for the rain comes."

She let Tuthmosis lead her back inside toward a comfortable-looking couch. Sitting down, she wiped her tears with her fingertips. "I am sorry, sire, for it is not in my nature to cry."

"You have every right to cry after what has happened to you," was his reply as he wiped a few stray tears off her cheek with the tip of his finger.

Seconds ticked by as they looked at each other, neither moving nor speaking. Then Tuthmosis slowly bent down and gently kissed her. Not wanting to frighten her, he drew back. She hid her face against him. Tiggy let him hold her in his arms. She guessed that he had sensed her need to be held and feel protected from the horrors that she had endured.

She eventually pulled back and shyly looked up at him. "I am sorry, sire, but thank you, for it was what I needed."

Caressing her cheek, he gently said, "Your thanks are not necessary."

Quietly, she inquired, "Shall I continue with the rest of the story?"

"Yes, I must know it, though I must admit I do not want to hear of you being treated in such a manner."

Leaning sideways on the couch, she faced him and began her story again. Quickly, she went through how she had been tied to a chair and how these men had cut her for being a foreigner in their land. "They were filled with such evil and hatred against me, sire. It was like someone had told them lies about me. They don't even know me, and yet they had this violent hatred for me. I don't understand. Also, why did they bring me back to the palace? I know very well that they could have killed me."

Tuthmosis's face was taut with anger. She reached out a tentative hand to touch him gently on the cheek. "Pharaoh, please do not be angry with me."

He started, looking directly at her. She watched as his gaze softened. "I am angry, but not at you. I am angry that someone would dare treat you in such a revolting manner. You should be treated like the princess that you are."

Rising to his feet, he said, "Come with me. I have something to give you that will help protect you when I am not able to be around you."

Taking her hand, Tuthmosis led her across his room into his bedchamber. They swiftly crossed it and went through a door, which led to a small room filled with wooden boxes. They were stacked on what appeared to be shelves. Tiggy thought that this room must be something like a closet. He went directly to a wide yet small wooden box. Opening it up, he drew out a necklace. Her eyes widened as she beheld the Nekhbet carved into a piece of gold hanging from a short, thick golden chain.

"It is beautiful, sire," she breathed as he came toward her. Reaching down, he pulled up her hands and placed the necklace in them.

"The workmanship is exquisite, but what is it for, sire?"

"It is for protection. The goddess will protect you from harm when I am not able to watch over you." Picking up the necklace again, he moved behind her. Pushing her hair aside, he gently kissed her neck and then placed the necklace around it. He hooked the clasp and let her hair cascade over her shoulders. "You enchant me like no other woman ever has."

"Sire, I—" she began as she turned in his arms, but they were interrupted by a pounding on the door. Both turned quickly toward the source of the sound. Instinctively, she moved to stand behind him, wanting his protection. She placed her hand on the back of his arm as they crossed into the main room.

She stopped and stood beside the couch as Tuthmosis proceeded to open the door. She watched as he talked to one of his magi. She was too far away to hear what was being said, but she did recognize the man from her abduction. She stepped into his line of vision as he bowed to the pharaoh. When he arose, she saw his eyes widen as he beheld the necklace she now wore around her neck. He gave the slightest of nods in her direction and quickly turned to leave.

Tiggy turned and walked toward the balcony as Tuthmosis shut the door behind him. She could hear him muttering as he crossed the room to stand beside her. Neither spoke as he reached her.

Tiggy stood silently as she watched the rain fall in torrents. A deep sigh escaped her as she looked out across the rain-drenched garden below. Her hand grasped the long silk curtain blowing in the breeze.

Finally, Tuthmosis broke into her reverie. "What are your thoughts?"

"I was just thinking of my home," she responded with an unwavering gaze. "I would stand, very much like I am standing now, in my rooms at home and watch as the heavens poured forth life to the earth. I love the smell of the rain and the cleansing it brings with it. I pray that cleansing will come from this."

"It shall," he reassured her as he took hold of her hand.

Turning toward him, she replied, looking into his eyes with warmth, "I must thank you for such a magnificent gift. I will treasure it always, because it was given to me from your hand." Reaching down, she placed it inside her dress. "I will wear it close to my heart and feel its touch as it still carries the warmth of your hands."

"It holds the warmth from my heart," he declared as he picked up her hand and placed it against his chest. Pulling her closer, he bent down and once again slowly kissed her. As she responded to him, he deepened their kiss.

Suddenly, the door slammed open. Both turned toward the sound, shocked to see Merira. "How dare you!" she screamed as she strode across the room toward them.

Still embracing the pharaoh, Tiggy drew closer to Tuthmosis as she saw the hatred on Merira's face.

"How dare you!" she screamed again as she stood before them. "You are my friend, and you do this to me? I gave you sanctuary from your father, and you try to steal my future husband from me."

Breaking from their embrace, Tiggy stood before her. "I am not trying to steal him from you," she replied calmly. Glancing briefly at him and then back to Merira, she quietly stated, "I have developed feelings for him. I have fought against them for your sake, but I cannot help it. You know that! You were there by the bathing pool when I told him that you were to be his God Wife, not me!"

111

"You lie!" she screamed back into her face. "You lied to me!"

"I didn't lie to you," retorted Tiggy. "It's just … well … when he kissed me, I felt …"

"Kissed you!" she screamed, and then, lifting her hand, she prepared to strike Tiggy across the face.

But Tiggy anticipated this and reached up and grabbed Merira's wrist firmly in her hand. In a quiet voice, she said, "You will not touch me." Roughly throwing down Merira's hand, Tiggy stepped from her toward Tuthmosis. Reaching out, she gently caressed his cheek; looking deeply into his eyes, she moved closer and tenderly kissed his lips. Stepping back, she looked up and said softly, while touching his face again, "Thank you for what you have done for me, sire. I will always remember it and you in my heart." Turning, she fled the room before either one of them could stop her.

CHAPTER SIXTEEN

▼

Closing the doors behind her, Tiggy heard a storm of hollering pouring forth from an incensed Tuthmosis that mimicked the storm that was raging around the palace. Quickly, Tiggy sped across the garden as the rain pelted her face and the wind tore at her clothes. Faster and faster she fled toward her room, intent on leaving this time as quickly as possible.

Moments later, she opened the doors to find Ian pacing the floor and Nikki standing beside their bundles, looking worried. Rushing across the room, she exclaimed, "Did they bring the bracelet?"

"Something was brought to your room," returned Ian, "but I didn't go to look at it."

Running across the room into her bedchamber, Tiggy spied the bracelet on her dressing table. Quickly, she clasped it on her arm and fled back out the room.

As she rushed toward the doors, Ian stopped her. "Where are you going?"

"I am going to walk the halls of the palace, for I have to be seen by Senenmut's guards with the bracelet on in order for us to be taken to the room where we are to leave."

"You're coming with me," said a voice from the balcony. "Time is fading quickly, for Princess Merira suspects what you possess." A man draped in black with his face covered stepped into the room. Ian drew out his gun, not caring who saw it or his attire. "Step back, Tiggy, Nikki. I'll handle this."

"No," interrupted Tiggy, putting out her hand, "he is one of Senenmut's guards." Grabbing her things, which Nikki had already packed, she extinguished most of the lights that were burning and turned to the man. "We are ready to go. Is everything ready?"

At her words, the door flew open, and there stood Merira, her face full of fury and her eyes full of hatred. "You shall die this night! You hold all the pieces, for I knew as you fled the pharaoh's room that you were leaving to claim what is mine! The treasure is mine," she screamed, "for I will take all the pieces from your dead body."

Ian moved to stand in front of Nikki and Tiggy with his gun raised, and Senenmut's guard stood beside him.

"You shall not harm the chosen one, or you will die," stated the guard, pulling his sword free from its sheath.

Ian, not understanding what the man said, knew that he meant to help them escape even at the cost of his own life.

Merira just began to laugh as she walked farther into the room. "You simple fools. You fell right into my trap, and now you shall all die."

"Not without a fight," declared Tiggy, raising her chin defiantly.

Laughing, Merira turned and simply said, "Come!"

Hessam and several of his men entered the room. As they drew their swords, Ian kept his gun focused on the group, watching as they shut and barred the doors against the pharaoh's guards that they knew would come. Ian waited, knowing that he had six shots—enough to take out most of Hessam's men.

At the moment, they were at a standstill, and the tension in the room was running high; the two groups faced the other, neither moving, just watching.

Then, as if Merira could no longer stand her anger, she swiftly turned and grabbed a small but vicious-looking sword from the wall. She screamed as she ran toward Tiggy. At the sound of her screams, which echoed above the raging of the storm, chaos erupted.

Tiggy, seeing Merira headed toward her, swiftly made for the far side of the room and pulled a sword off the wall.

Their swords clashed as the two women began to fight. All was at stake, and each of them knew it.

Ian began to shoot the men closest to them as Nikki grabbed the mate to Tiggy's sword and joined the fight.

For several minutes, the fighting continued as the sounds of the pharaoh's guards pounding upon the door could be heard above the chaos.

Merira screamed as Tiggy's sword sliced into the top of her arm. Again and again, their swords clashed, and at long last, Tiggy pinned Merira to the wall with the tip of her sword.

"Enough!" she screamed. "Call off your guards," Tiggy gasped between breaths. At Merira's silence, Tiggy pushed the tip of her sword against Merira's throat.

"Stop!" Merira finally spat out with naked fury burning in her eyes at having been beaten.

Slowly, Hessam and his men dropped their swords as the two groups looked at each other.

Looking around, Nikki saw the bodies of the men that Ian had shot first and shuddered at what had just occurred.

Seconds ticked by, and then unexpectedly, Hessam shouted, "No!" as he lunged at Tiggy, intending to kill her. But, just in time, Ian stepped forward with his sword and pierced Hessam right above the heart. Silence reigned as Hessam momentarily stood still with a shocked look upon his face and then fell to the floor.

"You traitor," declared Tiggy with hardened eyes and her sword tip still pressing into Merira's throat. "You killed your own mother to obtain her treasure. You murderer, you snake! You're beneath contempt, and you don't deserve the right to be called Hatshepsut's daughter!"

"You won't escape! Tuthmosis will hear of this!" retorted Merira through gritted teeth.

Nikki watched as Tiggy lowered her sword, and he saw the gleam of triumph that entered Merira's eyes. He knew by the look on Tiggy's face that she was not done.

Merira seized the opportunity and lunged forward with her sword. But Tiggy had anticipated this and neatly sidestepped her movement. With her sword, she knocked Merira's sword from her hand and watched as it spun across the floor to stop at Nikki's feet.

Having lost her weapon, Merira turned and rushed at Tiggy, who was waiting for her. Clenching her fist, Tiggy drew back and punched Merira full in the face, knocking her out.

"That's how we take care of people like you in America!" Tiggy announced as Merira slid to the floor at her feet.

Seeing that their fight was over, Nikki, Ian, and Senenmut's guard finished tying up the last of Hessam's men.

Turning, Ian told Nikki, "Get our things."

Without saying a word, Nikki crossed over to the balcony and retrieved their satchels and bags from where he had dropped them to the floor when the fight had begun.

Ian questioned Senenmut's man when he saw him knock Hessam's guards unconscious.

The man simply stated, "They must never know of the secret room of my master and Queen Hatshepsut."

Crossing the room, he nodded to everyone that it was time to go. Reaching high above a bronze wall ornament, he pushed in the head of the vulture. Slowly, a small, thin panel moved, allowing them access to a narrow passageway. "Bring the light," he stated.

Quickly, Ian grabbed a candle from his bag and lit it, dispelling the darkness. They traveled downward for several minutes before they reached a chamber that was painted blue with a ceiling covered with hundreds of white painted stars. "This is beautiful," said Tiggy.

The man nodded and smiled. "Senenmut built it for Hatshepsut as a place where they could share their love, away from the prying eyes of the court."

Tiggy nodded.

"Come, let us waste no time. Join the pieces, and travel back to your own time. Tell the people of the world of the greatness of Pharaoh Hatshepsut and Senenmut."

"We promise we will," declared Nikki, Ian, and Tiggy in unison.

Turning to Ian and Nikki, Tiggy declared, "Let's go home. Get out your pieces, and let's join them together. I don't know how long it will be before the pharaoh's guards get into that room and find all of the dead and unconscious bodies. We need to leave this place as quickly as possible."

"Yeah, let's get out of here," agreed Nikki as he pulled his two pieces from the little leather bag hidden within his shirt.

One by one, the gold pieces they had found were joined together like pieces of a puzzle, with Tiggy adding the thin gold "locks" that Senenmut had given her into their places. Finally, the last piece was placed, and the last lock was inserted.

Just as before, a bright light poured forth, the wind began to roar, and the sand on the floor began to swirl around them. "Here we go again," screamed out Nikki, somewhat frightened, as he had been before.

"Hold on, everyone," shouted Ian as he grabbed hold of Tiggy and Nikki.

Through the shifting sand and the bright light, Tiggy looked up to see Senenmut standing on the stairs with tears on his face. He raised his hand in farewell as she momentarily let go of Ian's arm to raise hers in return. She shouted loudly to him, "I will not forget my promise to you. I will not!" The wind roared louder and the light intensified, and Tiggy could see him no more. The wind began to pull and push on them as it had before. Finally the sand stopped swirling and the wind stopped roaring. The light began to fade, and only Tiggy's amulet continued to glow.

Ian found his voice first. "Is everyone all right?" he said, rising to his feet from where he had been lying on the ground.

"Did it work?" asked Nikki, rolling over on his side where he lay in the sand.

"I have no idea," replied Tiggy, somewhat disoriented, as she too rose to her feet and brushed the sand from her pants. As Ian relit the candle that had been extinguished by the wind, she glanced around the room. "It looks like the same room we were just in," cried out Nikki in dismay.

"It is, Nikki," said Ian, "but look at the walls. They are covered with the dust of the ages. Let's just hope that we returned to our own time."

Ian helped Tiggy place the pieces, which were still joined together, around her neck for safekeeping. Then they began to climb the stairs. Upon reaching the top landing, both Ian and Nikki tried to move the door, but they were unsuccessful.

"Look for a handle or a key," announced Ian.

Feeling around on the walls, Nikki declared, "Shine the light over here. I think I found something."

Both Tiggy and Ian shone their lights on the spot where Nikki had placed his hand.

"The amulet," gasped Tiggy. Leaning over Nikki's arm, she placed the amulet that she wore around her neck into the spot. "It fits!" she declared happily. Pushing it in, she turned it counterclockwise and then pushed it farther inward. While she was still pushing, the thin panel began to slide open. Finally, it opened far enough for the three of them to slip out. Stepping into the room they had been in only moments before, each looked around with a mixture of jubilation and sorrow, for before their eyes the once-magnificent room lay in ruins.

Several moments passed before Nikki recalled them from their thoughts. "Come on, you two. We have to see if we came back to the right time." Rushing toward the door, he left Ian and Tiggy to follow him.

Having been in the palace for several days, each knew the way to their base camp. Minutes later, they arrived at the upper ramp.

"Yes," cried out Nikki, jumping up and down, unable to contain his joy. "We're back!"

"Thank you, Lord. That's over with," declared a reverent Ian.

"Yes," agreed Tiggy quietly.

Nikki, running on ahead, screamed out, "Come on, you guys. I am starving for some real food."

Tiggy and Ian looked at each and began to laugh. Making their way more slowly down the ramp, Ian asked, "One day, will you tell me what really happened?" At her look of confusion, he added, "I mean, the parts that were in Egyptian and we could not understand."

"Yes, but only if you fill in the gaps that I have."

Ian reached out his hand and grasped her, saying, "I am glad to have you back."

"Me too," echoed Tiggy.

"Now, let's go get some food, for we still have that treasure to find," declared Ian, not letting go of her hand as they made their way down the ramp.

Minutes later, they joined Nikki at the camp. He was way ahead of them, already stuffing his face. They just sat down, laughing at the sight he made.

"You act like you haven't eaten anything good in days," said Ian mischievously.

"Well, I practically haven't," he replied between mouthfuls. "Tiggy, when are we going to look for the treasure?"

"How about tomorrow?" she said, reaching out to take her food from Ian.

"How about we return to Luxor tomorrow and come back with more supplies, more camels, and fewer men?" ventured Ian.

Pausing in the wake of his words, Tiggy thought that his suggestion made perfect sense. "I agree," she returned.

"But why do we need to wait?" retorted Nikki. "It's not like Merira is a threat anymore."

"This is true," agreed Ian, "but we don't want the workers trying to steal our treasure either, if we find it."

"Do we even know where to begin?" questioned Nikki.

"Well, that's a good question," replied Tiggy. "Let's see if I can answer that. Reaching down, she drew out the pieces that made the map and glanced at it. It glowed with a beautiful golden light that had nothing to do with the afternoon sun. She also drew out the amulet and felt its warmth. They all marveled when she turned it over and began reading the hieroglyphics.

"Yes, it does tell us exactly where to find the hidden wealth. It's very specific, even to the point of telling exactly how many steps to this wall and to this column: how many steps downward, about a step of courage, and many other things. And of course, there's also a curse to any that are not with the chosen one, for they surely will die a horrible death. You know … the usual scary things."

"Can we just go and see if the treasure is there and then leave in the morning?" inquired Nikki.

"I don't see why not," replied Tiggy. "I'm willing if Ian is."

"I've no problem with that," he responded.

"All right then. Let's finish eating and then go searching for it," she declared with enthusiasm.

Fifteen minutes later, the three began their trek back up the two ramps that led to the upper colonnade. Once inside the third court area, Nikki looked around the large rectangular room that was decorated floor to ceiling with hieroglyphics. Gone were the polished floors, the golden statues, and the magi on duty. "Kind of sad to see it like this," stated Nikki.

"Yes, it is," vaguely returned Tiggy while glancing at the map. "It says that we must go into the Shrine of Anubis."

Nikki led the way down the long corridor until they reached the shrine's entrance. "Which way do we go now?"

"It says to take twenty footsteps to the west of the entrance."

"Which entrance?" asked Ian. "The entrance to the shrine or the entrance to the whole temple?"

"I've no idea," Tiggy said. "Just try both ways, and see what you find."

Ian began to mark off twenty steps in one direction with no luck. With the second try, he found success. "I can see a replica of the amulet you're wearing around your neck.

"Maybe this is it," cried out Nikki.

"No, this would be too easy," declared Tiggy with disbelief. Taking the necklace off, she placed it in the wall and began to push it inward. Slowly, a section of the wall began to move.

Ian stood there in disbelief. "These people never cease to amaze me with what they were capable of doing. That door must easily weigh over a thousand pounds, yet a simple locking mechanism moves it back and forth. Incredible."

Ian reached over and lit a torch that was on the wall, and Tiggy began their downward descent.

Minutes later, Nikki asked, "How much farther? It's getting cold down here, and it stinks too. "

"I've no idea. It just says that we will come to a column, and from there, we are supposed to turn to left and have courage. "

"I swear these people were all into courage and not into making things easier for other people to find," complained Nikki as he kicked several crawling bugs from his path.

"That's the point," laughed Ian. "They don't want to make it easy to find their treasure. Would you?"

"No, I guess not," said Nikki, grimacing, as he swatted at something that flew past his head.

"Look ... up ahead is the column, and the passageway splits in two," declared Tiggy. "We're to take the one on the left."

Turning to the left, they began to descend into a steeper, narrower passageway.

"Whoa, this is really getting steep," exclaimed Nikki as he slipped and fell.

Ian reached down and picked Nikki up, saying, "Are you sure this is the way? This keeps going downward."

"That's what the map is telling me."

"I have a bad feeling about this," said Nikki as he heard the sound of something rustling, and the flame flickered and almost went out with a sudden and startling whoosh of the wind.

"What's that noise?" asked Nikki in a frightened voice.

"I've no idea, but that wind came out of nowhere!" said Ian with a worried voice.

"You don't suppose it is Merira, do you, Tiggy?" asked Nikki, his voice cracking.

"I don't know. Senenmut never said anything about her ability to follow us. I really don't want to see her again after what happened."

"I didn't hear the wind say anything," stated Ian.

"Well, let's just hope that it's an air current that runs through the passage. Come on," stated Tiggy as she turned around and continued down the passage.

Minutes later, even she was beginning to have her doubts and concerns about the depth of their descent.

Finally, she exclaimed, "We must have gone too far." At her words, the wind roared down the passage, swirling around them again and again and blowing sand up into their faces.

Closing their eyes, they tried to get away from it. It kept pushing them until they were turned completely around. Then suddenly it stopped.

Breathing hard, each looked at the others, with faces full of worry and concern.

"Merira," Nikki squeaked out.

"I don't know," managed Tiggy, trying to catch her breath. "I didn't hear anything."

"That couldn't have been just the wind," stated Ian, brushing the sand from his eyes with a worried look.

All three were frightened by the possibility that Merira had been able to follow them.

Turning around to look down the passage, Tiggy noticed a bright glow that seemed to come from the ground.

Everyone began to back up as it became brighter and brighter. Their eyes widened with fear. Then a strong, gentle voice spoke, a voice that Tiggy recognized as Senenmut's.

"The map … make sure of the map." And with a flash, the light was gone, and the passageway ahead was once again engulfed in darkness.

"What the heck was that?" questioned Nikki in a startled voice.

"That was Senenmut," declared Tiggy. "I think he's trying to tell us that we must be doing something wrong. We must not be reading the map right."

"Then let's take a break. Tiggy, you check out the map," stated Nikki, sitting down in the sandy passage.

"I agree," said Tiggy with concern. Sitting down in the sand, she began to study the map in further detail.

"Find anything?" questioned Ian as he sat down next to her.

"I don't know," she returned with a puzzled look. "There seems to be some inconsistencies in the map."

"What do you mean?"

"I don't know," she returned as she examined the map. "Do you have your magnifying glass handy?"

Ian nodded; turning to his bag, he pulled out the glass.

"Here you go."

"What are you looking for?" inquired Nikki.

"I don't know ... I just don't know ..." said Tiggy as her words trailed off. "But there must be something, because Senenmut wants us to check the map." Pausing, she put her eye closer to the glass. "Hmmm."

"What is it?" asked Ian.

"Here. Hold the magnifying glass while I do something."

Reaching out, Ian took the magnifying glass from her hand.

"Nikki, lean the light more this way. There is a shadow."

"What do you see?" asked Ian again as she bent closer to the map.

"Can you see that the hieroglyphics are slightly off?" she said, pointing to one of them.

"Yes, they look somewhat distorted," agreed Ian.

"That's what intrigues me, because the Egyptians were exact in almost everything, especially their workmanship."

Tiggy cautiously pulled on one of the locks while watching the hieroglyphics. Slowly, she began to twist the lock as she saw the images begin to change.

"Will you look at that?" declared Ian in awe and disbelief.

"What?" said Nikki, peering over their heads. "I can't see."

"Watch it, will you?" cried out Ian as he touched his cheek. "You almost burned me with the torch."

"Sorry!" Nikki returned as he continued to stretch to see what Tiggy was doing.

"That's it! I've got to turn the locks!" she cried out. "Ooh, that was really clever. I am impressed!"

Nikki and Ian watched as she turned the two locks. The hieroglyphics changed before their eyes. The entire map took on a new form.

"It's a totally different map!" Ian said in amazement.

"I don't think that we are through yet," responded Tiggy as she turned the map over.

"What do you mean?" asked Nikki.

"Look what just appeared on the back," she said, holding the back of the map for them to see.

"The amulet!" cried Ian.

"Exactly," she said with a nod. "Senenmut told me it would be vital in finding the treasure, but even he did not know how it would be used, just that I would know at the journey's end."

Carefully, she placed the amulet into the back of the gold map. As she had done with everything else, she began to turn it until she could turn it no more. Flipping it over, she stared at the front, for it had changed yet again.

"Can you believe it?" declared Ian.

"No, I can't," returned Tiggy, sitting in the sand with an incredulous look on her face.

"We would have gone on all kinds of wild goose chases," joined in Nikki, "and we probably would have never found it."

"You're probably right," said Tiggy. "We probably would have thought the treasure had been discovered and pilfered through the ages."

"Where does the map take us now?" ventured Ian.

Tiggy began reading the text and finally nodded her head. "Hatshepsut's royal vizier was one exceptionally cunning man."

"Why do you say that?"

"According to this, the treasure is hidden in the suite of rooms allotted to the pharaoh's wife. Those rooms would have belonged to Hatshepsut and later to Merira."

"You're kidding!" said Ian incredulously.

"No, I am not," said Tiggy, laughing. "Just think: the treasure was so close to Merira, and she never even knew it."

"Where is the entrance to the chamber? Does it say?" asked Ian.

"Yes, it does. It says that the entrance is in the bathing room. Now that I think about it, part of the room goes into the mountain, and that would be the perfect place to hide a treasure."

"Well, come on then," said Nikki, jumping to his feet. "Let's go find it."

"Yes. We should probably get out of this passageway, for I don't like the sound of that rustling noise," Ian exclaimed as he heard the scurrying sound again.

Forty minutes later, Ian, Nikki, and Tiggy arrived at what used to be Princess Merira's royal suites. "You would never imagine that this is the same room we saw just a few hours ago," stated Tiggy as she looked around at the crumbling walls, noting the absence of gold, silk, and polished granite floors.

"Nikki," said Ian, "hand me your torch, for the sun is sinking low on the horizon, and soon it will be dark."

Nikki handed his torch to Ian and waited for him to light it as Tiggy combed the walls, looking for the amulet.

After a few minutes, she said, "Everyone spread out on this wall and look for the amulet design. It has to be the key to open the door that will lead to the treasure."

Fanning out, they quickly covered every inch of the wall.

Dismayed, Nikki said, "I don't see anything that looks like that sun design you're wearing. All I have over here is a sluice of some sort. I guess it was used to bring water in for bathing."

"Ian, do you have anything?" inquired Nikki.

"No, nothing here."

"Me neither," declared Tiggy disappointedly. "Maybe we should come back when the light is not fading."

"No," cried Nikki, "it has to be here. Let's just try a little longer."

Ian and Tiggy looked at each other and nodded their agreement. "All right, Nikki," said Ian. "Twenty minutes more, tops. Agreed?"

"Yes," was the reluctant reply.

"Where are you going?" asked Ian as he spied Tiggy heading across the room.

"Oh, I am just going to take a look over here."

Ian nodded and then continued to look with Nikki. "You look low, Nikki, and I will look higher."

Tiggy went across the room and began to stare at the wall, trying to see it through the eyes of someone who hid things in plain sight. It did not take her long to see that the area where the sluice came through the wall was in the design of a circle with two rays shooting off. "I have it!" she declared.

Quickly turning around, both Ian and Nikki exclaimed, "Where?"

Pointing to where they were standing, she triumphantly said, "There— right where the two of you are standing, only you can't see it because you are too close to it. Look on the sluice. There has to be a sun on one of the sluices."

"Yes, there is," declared Ian excitedly. "It is on the underside."

"Then we have it!" crowed Nikki with joy.

"I sure hope this is it," stated Tiggy as she crossed the room and bent down to see the design on the sluice. Taking off the amulet, she placed it into the design and began to turn it. Sure enough, a small section of the wall below the sluice began to groan open. The more she turned it, the more the door slid open. Finally, she could turn it no more.

"Are we ready for this?' asked Ian with a rather apprehensive look.

After taking a deep breath, Tiggy said, "I think I'm ready for this, after all we've been through."

Turning to Nikki, Ian inquired the same of him.

"Definitely!"

"All right then," breathed Ian. "You first, Tiggy, for you are the one that is supposed to find it."

Taking a breath, she said, "Here we go."

Putting the torch through the opening under the sluice, she crawled for the first five or six feet. After that, she could see that the passageway widened and became taller. Standing, she turned around to wait for Ian and Nikki to follow.

"It's all clear here," she hollered. Seconds later, Nikki emerged, followed by Ian.

"Where now?" asked Ian.

Taking out the map, Tiggy glanced at the hieroglyphics. "It says to follow the path of the rising sun."

"Path of the sun? Inside what's basically a mountain?" asked Ian.

"That's what it says."

"But that doesn't make sense," cried Nikki.

"Well, it might if we keep going," retorted Tiggy as she began walking ahead. "Look at the beautiful drawings rendered on this passage. They're not painted. They're filled in with gold!"

Ian suddenly stopped and declared, "Yes, look closely at the drawings. They are showing people carrying treasure."

Both Tiggy and Nikki stopped to look at the drawings.

"Oh," cried Nikki, "I hope that's really real."

"I think we all do, Nikki," she responded as she continued walking.

"Tiggy, what's that smell?" asked Nikki.

"That's the smell of stale air. Just think: if the air smells like this, then we can be sure that none have entered this passageway for thousands of years."

Yards away from the opening, they came to passageway that was perpendicular to theirs. Stopping, Tiggy looked both ways and pondered whether to keep going or to turn to the left or to the right.

"Which way?" questioned Ian.

"Follow the path of the sun," reminded Nikki.

"Yes, I know," responded Tiggy. "But look—each passageway has a sun on the corner."

"Hmm, that does pose a problem," mused Ian.

Nikki suddenly had an idea. "Hey, Ian. Do you have your compass?"

"Yes, I do. Why?"

"Well, the sun rises in the east and sets in the west."

"True," agreed Ian.

"So, maybe we should go to the east along the passageway and then finish in the west."

"It can't hurt," declared Tiggy, "because the map does not say anything that would help us."

"All right," agreed Ian as he took out his compass. "We're already going east, so let's just turn to the west and keep walking."

After a few minutes, Tiggy questioned Ian, "Does it seem like we are walking on an incline?"

"Yes, it does," he confirmed. "A slight one, but one nonetheless."

Suddenly, Ian exclaimed, "Look at the size of that door!"

Pausing, all three looked in awe at the enormity of the door before them.

"This has to be it," shouted Nikki. "It just has to be."

Walking up to it, Tiggy placed her hand against the handles. Resting her head against the door, she began to feel detached from herself. She closed her eyes and could see the image of Senenmut before her. When she opened her eyes again, he was there before her.

"You have done well," he said with a nod as she smiled at him; she was unafraid, knowing he would not harm her. "I knew that you were the one who would find our treasure. We will live on. I know that we can trust you to do what is right and good—that you will share this knowledge of a great and powerful woman with your world."

"We can and we will do all that is within our power. I have given you my word."

Glancing to his left, Tiggy could see a beautiful and proud woman. She knew at once by her proud stance and her welcoming smile that before her stood Queen Hatshepsut. Overwhelmed and awestruck, Tiggy sank to the ground in a proper curtsy as the great pharaoh queen approached her.

Reaching down, Queen Hatshepsut grasped Tiggy's hands and pulled her to her feet. "I owe you much," she said as she looked at Tiggy. "You and you as well"—her glance shifted to include Ian and Nikki—"have done and will do much to preserve my legacy. I will give you my thanks for all eternity, and now we must go. We both can go in peace, knowing that our lives have truly been completed." After kissing Tiggy on both cheeks, she and Senenmut suddenly vanished.

For a moment, none of them moved. Finally, Tiggy asked, "Did you see them too?"

"Yes," replied Ian faintly, finding his voice at last.

Nikki just nodded his head, too stunned to speak.

"Then I guess that this is really it," she said with a wide smile, overcoming her immobility at the queen's appearance and disappearance.

Taking the amulet from around her neck, she fit it into the impression below the handle and began to turn it. With a faint whoosh, the doors began to open slowly. Standing side by side, all three walked into the doorway, holding their torches high.

Their eyes widened as they glimpsed only what their torchlight could reveal: great piles of gold, jewels, statues, furniture, and treasure that rivaled anything ever found anywhere upon the earth.

Nikki broke the silence by demanding, "Come on, you two. We've got a lot of work to do."

With a laugh, Ian and Tiggy followed her, filled with joy at what they finally had discovered after such a long and arduous journey.

Tiggy stopped; glancing behind, she saw the images of Hatshepsut and Senenmut, nodding their heads in approval. Raising her hand, she waved as their images faded into the walls of time. *Yes indeed*, she thought as she turned to go, *we do have a lot of work to do in presenting the marvelous treasure and life of a great female pharaoh named Hatshepsut to the world.*

Egyptian Terms/Symbols

amulet: A charm, often in the form of hieroglyphs, gods, or sacred animals, made of precious stones or materials. They were worn like jewelry during life and were included within the mummy wrappings for the afterlife.

ankh: A hieroglyphic sign symbolizing life.

auta: The name for the cobra in the striking position represented on the crowns of the pharaohs.

barque: A royal boat used by ancient Egyptians to transport statues of gods or mummies.

cartouche: An oval figure in ancient Egyptian hieroglyphics that encloses characters expressing the names of rulers or gods.

lotus flower: Really a water lily but used to symbolize the union of Upper and Lower Egypt.

Nekhbet: The vulture goddess of Upper Egypt; the protector of the king.

Pharaoh's crook: The crook showed that the pharaoh was the protector and ruler of all the people.

scarab: An ancient Egyptian fertility symbol based on a common dung beetle found in Egypt. It was often carried as an amulet cast from gold or carved from semiprecious stones.

Made in the USA
Lexington, KY
11 November 2014